Lie Detectives

Without warning, a dark car seemed to rev from a standstill to an instant eighty kilometres an hour and it came racing towards Bullet, who had now reached the middle of the road. Theo was the first to see it.

"NO!" Theo yelled a warning.

"Bullet, look out!"

Bullet turned his head and saw the car racing towards him. Shock froze him to the tarmac. Ricky leapt forward – but Angela beat him to it. She dashed into the middle of the road, just as the car was almost upon Bullet and shoved him out of the way. Angela tried to dive after him, but she wasn't so lucky. The side of the car hit her and Angela was knocked into the air. And in that moment, Theo's heart stopped beating.

MALORIE BLACKMAN

Lie Detectives

Hippo

Scholastic Children's Books,
Commonwealth House,
1-19 New Oxford Street,
London WC1A 1NU, UK
A division of Scholastic Ltd
London ~ New York ~ Toronto ~ Sydney ~ Auckland

First published in the UK by Scholastic Ltd, 1998

Copyright © Oneta Malorie Blackman, 1998

ISBN 0 590 13429 9

Typeset by
Cambrian Typesetters, Frimley, Camberley, Surrey
Printed by
Cox and Wyman Ltd, Reading, Berks

10 9 8 7 6 5 4 3 2 1

For Neil and Elizabeth
with love

Prologue

" Are we really going to go through with this?"

The night rain battered at the window as if trying to get through it. The woman sipped her mineral water, unable to disguise the way her hand was shaking. The ice in her drink clinked and clinked again against the sides of her glass. She could almost imagine it was beating out a coded message.

Don't do it! Don't do it!

She put the glass down with a bump, some of its contents sloshing out on to the coffee table. She stood up to close the curtains. They should've been closed ages ago. Even though this flat was on the second floor of the tallest building for streets around, she still felt nervous about the possibility of being watched. Usually she closed the curtains before she even switched on the lights in the flat. She wasn't usually so careless. They had agreed that they couldn't take any chances. It wasn't like her. She turned around.

"Is there really no other way?" she whispered.

The man shook his head. "You know there isn't. We don't have any choice. This latest invention of his is milking the company dry. If we don't stop him — and soon — the company will be worth about ten pence, if we're lucky. DemTech is just as much ours as it is his."

"Couldn't we ... fight him in court or something?"

"Darling, we've been through all this before. On paper DemTech belongs to him. In court we wouldn't have a leg to stand on. And d'you think I'd be suggesting we do this if there was any other way?" the man replied softly. "He's taken over financial control of this project himself so I can't find out what it's really costing the company, but I know it's a lot more than he's stated publicly. We've both worked too long and too hard to let DemTech go down the drain now."

The woman sighed her agreement but her expression was far from happy. She sat down next to the man on the settee. "I'm scared. I think ... I think he may know about us..."

The man raised a sceptical eyebrow.

"Don't look at me like that," the woman argued. "I'm telling you, he's on to us."

"What makes you think that?"

"Over the last couple of days he's been making some very peculiar comments. Strange comments – about you and how hard you work and about me and how he wouldn't have got this far without me fighting at his side and in his corner. Stuff like that."

"Maybe he means it."

"Yeah, right!"

The man poured himself some mineral water from the bottle on the table. "OK. What else?"

"Someone logged on to my computer earlier today and went through most of my files. That's why I wanted to see you tonight."

The man sat bolt upright. "Did they get...?"

"Don't worry. I'm not that stupid. I removed all our stuff from my computer a couple of days ago."

"And you reckon Darius was the one who logged on to your computer?"

"Who else would have access to it?"

The man wiped a hand over his forehead. "We'll need to act fast then – just in case. He's going on some ridiculous school visit tomorrow which should prove the ideal time and place to ... to get him out of the way."

"Tomorrow?" the woman said, aghast. "So soon?"

"Darling, look at us. Look at the way we live. Sneaking around corners and hiding like criminals when we've done nothing wrong. And it's all thanks to Darius Marriott and his ridiculous will. I can't even tell my family about you because of him. I'm sick and tired of living this way."

"So am I, but this is so ... so ... *final*." The

woman took a deep breath to try and control herself. "Once we've done this, there's no turning back."

"I know. That's why I have to know that you're beside me on this. I have to know I can count on you."

The woman bowed her head. Silent moments passed. When she looked up, her expression was no happier but it now held resolve. "If there's no other way..."

The man smiled his relief. "There isn't. We can't afford to hang about for much longer – not if he really does suspect something. I just need to know that the Lazarus suit will do what we want it to do." The man continued to whisper even though they were quite alone.

"That part of it is fine. It's all been set up. We just need to make sure that one of us is close enough to set it off," the woman replied.

They watched each other for several tense seconds.

"Are you sure there's no other way?" the woman asked again.

"I'm positive. We've got to get him out of the way once and for all."

"OK. I trust you, you know that." The woman sighed.

"Darling, think of it. We can be together openly. We won't have to creep off to another city once a week just to be together."

"I know. But I don't want anything to go wrong..."

"It won't. No one knows about us – no one. And by this time next week, Darius will be gone for good and you and I will own DemTech. And most important of all, we can be together openly, without all this sneaking around."

"I wish I had your confidence." The woman shook her head.

"Don't worry, I have enough confidence for both of us. This time tomorrow, Darius Marriott will be out of the picture – permanently."

1. Detecting Lies!

"**I**s that it then?" Theo whispered. Bullet nodded.

"Does it work?"

"I don't know," Bullet admitted. "I only finished it late last night."

Theo leaned in closer. Bullet held a rectangular gizmo about the size of a large calculator. It gave off a faint hissing sound like an untuned radio. It consisted of ten buttons numbered zero to nine, two small dials and an LCD screen which took up at least a third of the gadget. A small antenna stuck out of the top of the gizmo.

"What's that?" Angela, who sat on the

other side of Bullet, pointed to the contraption in Bullet's hands.

"A lie detector," Theo supplied before Bullet could open his mouth.

"What's it for?" asked Angela.

Bullet and Theo exchanged a look. "Detecting lies?" Theo suggested.

Angela's face flamed as Theo and Bullet exchanged another wry look. "Theo, there's no need to be quite so sarky."

"Then don't ask stupid questions!" Theo grinned.

"It wasn't a stupid question..." Angela was beginning to raise her voice now.

"Shush, you two. Before you have all the teachers over here," Bullet whispered.

Theo and Angela both sat back abruptly in their chairs. Theo had a quick glance around. Bullet was right. They were already getting a disapproving frown from Mr Cross – cross by name and cross by nature! Theo looked away, only to catch sight of Mrs Daltry scowling at them. Oops! Quickly, Theo looked up at the stage, wondering for how much longer this assembly was going to go on. They'd only been in the hall about ten minutes, which was nine minutes too long as far as Theo was concerned. Mrs Nash, the deputy head, was half-way through reading out the school announcements.

"What happens when your machine detects a lie?" Theo whispered out of the side of his mouth.

"It bleeps, unless I turn the sound off first. And it's got a built-in microtape recorder to record conversations and there's a recording chip in it which records the exact moment or moments in the conversation when lies were told," Bullet explained. "This lie detector can monitor a person up to ten metres away, it can record conversations of up to thirty minutes and it can indicate the sentences that are untrue."

"Does it sweep the floor as well?" Theo raised a sceptical eyebrow.

"Does it work?" Angela couldn't help asking.

"As I said, it's not fully tested yet but there's no reason why it shouldn't."

"And just how does it know when

someone's lying or not?" Theo asked, after looking around to make sure none of the teachers could see them talking.

"When people lie, they change the way they speak without realizing they're doing it. Their words might become faster or slower, or higher or lower. Of course, the closer I am to the person being tested, the better it works and the more accurate the results. It's similar in principle to a voice stress analyser except my invention is much more sophisticated."

Theo sniffed but said nothing. That was Bullet! As modest as ever!

"But once someone knows you're checking to see whether or not they're lying, they can change the way they tell their lies so that they fool your machine," said Ricky, leaning across Theo.

"That's why it's better if the person I'm testing doesn't know they're being tested," Bullet explained. "It also uses Doppler radar techniques to detect and monitor body changes. Then this lie detector interprets all the data..."

"This is turning into a Heathrow job," Theo sighed.

"Huh?"

"This is going over my head!" explained Theo. "But it'll be interesting to see if it works."

"Of course it works. *I* made it," sniffed Bullet.

"So who are you hoping to catch out in a lie?" Angela asked.

"No one in particular. I'm just testing it. I thought I'd try it out on our new headmaster," Bullet whispered back.

"Mr Unbar?" Angela said, surprised. "What d'you reckon he's lying about?"

"He's a grown-up and a teacher. So he's bound to lie at least once every five minutes," Bullet shrugged. He continued to fiddle with his gizmo.

"That's a bit cynical, isn't it?" Angela raised her eyebrows.

"After everything you've been through with your brother, I'd have thought you'd be the first to agree with me," said Bullet.

Angela didn't answer. She turned away to

stare straight ahead. Theo gave Bullet an angry look.

"What did you have for breakfast this morning? Tactless on toast?" said Theo.

Bullet looked at him, surprised. Then he turned to Angela. "Sorry. I didn't mean that the way it came out."

"Never mind. It doesn't matter," Angela shrugged.

"Angela, are you OK?" Theo asked, concerned.

"Yes, I'm fine."

Bullet looked down at his gizmo which was pointing in Angela's direction. A downward arrow flashed intermittently on it.

"What does that mean?" Theo pointed.

"Angela's lying," Bullet whispered in Theo's ear. He turned back to Angela. "I really am sorry. Sometimes my mouth gets to work before my brain has had a chance to kick in."

"OK," Angela nodded. The faint trace of a smile on her face disappeared as swiftly as it had appeared.

Theo gave Angela one last look before

turning back to the stage. Angela still didn't speak about her brother Tom much, even after all this time. Her brother was still in prison and Angela was the one who'd put him there. No wonder she couldn't bear to talk about him. Bullet should've known better.

"And now I have a wonderful surprise for all of you," said Mr Unbar as he took over from Mrs Nash up on the stage.

"Yeah, right!" Theo muttered. What their new headmaster thought was a wonderful surprise and what Theo might think was a wonderful surprise were bound to be two different things. Theo didn't need Bullet's lie detector to spot that little fib.

"As part of our school's policy to have visits from prominent people in industry, we are very lucky to have Mr Darius Marriott here with us today," the headmaster continued.

Bullet sat bolt upright and stared up at the stage as if he'd been stung. Well, maybe not stung – Bullet was allergic to wasp stings – but slapped at any rate. Theo frowned as he looked at Bullet. He'd never seen such a look of intense concentration and excitement on Bullet's face before – not even when Bullet had finally managed to get his program to solve crimes working.

"Darius Marriott, as I'm sure most of you already know, is the head of DemTech Industries. Over the last decade, his company has invented at least half of the new labour-saving devices we have in our homes today. DemTech are also leaders when it comes to medical, technological and military innovations."

At the few murmurs of distinct disapproval floating around the hall, Mr Unbar continued hastily. "And another division of his company invented the now classic game Operation StarBlaster."

The murmurs of disapproval were now mixed with whispers of appreciation and anticipation. Theo gave a sniff of derision. Mr Unbar never used one word where fifteen would do. If he meant that DemTech invented loads of gadgets used in hospitals and by the army then why didn't he just come right out and say so.

"So let's give him a big welcome," Mr Unbar smiled.

The hall erupted into spontaneous applause as a tall man wearing a white shirt and navy blue cords came on to the stage. Beneath his shirt but clearly visible, he wore a strange-looking black-grey waistcoat or vest with sleeves down to his elbows.

"Hello everyone," Darius Marriott said with a smile. "I'm here today because I'm hoping to convince all of you of how wonderful science is! I'm hoping that some of you will become scientists and maybe some of you will come and work for my company."

Theo switched off. He didn't want to be a scientist. He wanted to be a famous detective, more famous than Sherlock Holmes and Hercule Poirot and Miss Marple put together. He'd be a private detective with swish offices somewhere in Central London and all the major cities around the world. He'd have a number of other private detectives working for him, but he'd be the best. He'd be so famous, he'd be on chat shows and in the papers and people would come to him to solve their most perplexing cases.

Ladies and gentlemen, it gives me great pleasure to introduce as my next guest Sir Theo Mosley – the greatest detective of the 21st century. The greatest detective the world has ever seen!

Theo drifted away, imagining the big house he'd buy and the plush offices he'd work from and all the money he'd have in his Swiss bank account until a sharp elbow in his ribs brought him back to reality. He glared at Ricky who grinned back at him.

"Now can anyone guess what I'm wearing under my shirt?" asked Darius Marriott, looking around the hall.

Darius proceeded to unbutton his shirt and take it off so that everyone could have a better look at the waistcoat underneath. Nervous giggles sprung up around the hall. The teachers gave each other dubious looks.

"Don't be shy!" Darius smiled. "What am I wearing?"

Silence. Then a couple of hands were

raised tentatively in the air. A few more hands went up. Darius pointed to Angela, who was one of the brave ones.

"Is it a bullet-proof vest?"

Theo wasn't the only one to burst out laughing. What a ridiculous answer! Trust Angela!

"You've been watching too many James Bond films!" Ricky leaned across Theo and Bullet to whisper to Angela.

"It might be," Angela defended herself.

"Actually that's a very good guess," said Darius, looking around. "And this suit uses similar technology for some of its components."

The laughter died down. Angela looked around with a vindicated, smug smile on her face.

"But it's not right," Darius Marriott continued. "How about you? What d'you think it is?"

"Is it for concealing things?"

"No."

"Is it some kind of jet pack for flying above the traffic?"

"No. But I wish it was," Darius Marriott smiled. "What a good idea!"

"Is it an invisibility suit?"

Theo gave a snort of derision. He turned his head, craning his neck to see who had come up with that daft idea. The guesses were growing more and more bizarre! Bullet put up his hand.

Darius Marriott pointed at him. "Yes?"

"Is it some kind of medical device?"

"What makes you say that?"

"It's the sleeves really," said Bullet. "They only go down to your elbows which makes me wonder if somehow they're for taking your blood pressure, 'cause they always take your blood pressure at about heart level."

"Well done! When you leave university you must apply for a job at my company," Darius Marriott smiled.

Theo gave Bullet a congratulatory dig in the ribs. Unfortunately, Angela chose that precise moment to do exactly the same thing. Bullet doubled over as if he'd been punched in the stomach.

"Are you OK?" Darius Marriott asked, concerned.

Bullet sat up, wincing as he breathed. "Yeah, I'm fine."

Theo caught sight of Mrs Daltry glowering at him and Angela. He sighed. He didn't have to be Einstein to know that the moment they were out of the hall, Mrs Daltry was going to have a rant.

"What I'm wearing is the result of a new project my company is working on called the Lazarus project. Lazarus was a man who, according to the Bible, was brought back to life by Jesus. We call this a Lazarus suit – even though really it's only a Lazarus waistcoat or jacket at best. But Lazarus suit sounds so much better, doesn't it?"

More than a few nods and smiles agreed with Darius.

"In fact some of you may have seen me talking about this Lazarus suit last week on the telly. Or perhaps some of you have seen articles about the Lazarus suit in the national papers? It was formally announced two weeks ago. And you'll have to forgive the poetic licence," Darius continued. "This device is well named because that's what the suit ultimately sets out to do. Another good name for it would be the suit of life. Our suit is designed to be worn by those who might need medical attention literally at a moment's notice. This Lazarus suit can take your blood pressure and monitor your heart rate. It can even administer medicines and some medical treatments. And what's more ... what's..." Darius Marriott's voice slowed and trailed off altogether. His eyes became glassy and he began to sway backwards and forwards.

Mr Unbar, the headmaster, stood up slowly, a frown on his face. "Mr Marriott, is everything all right?"

Darius Marriott tried for a smile and missed by several kilometres. "I ... I..." Then he suddenly lurched like a puppet being yanked off the ground before falling over on to his side. All the teachers sprang up at once and they weren't the only ones. Bullet leapt to his feet, his gizmo still hissing and crackling in his hand. Mr Unbar rushed over to Darius Marriott, who now lay still on the stage floor. Theo didn't know what to do, what to say. Was this a joke?

"Is this part of Mr Marriott's demonstration?" Angela whispered.

"I don't know," Theo replied slowly. "But I don't think so. I think this is real."

Murmurs and anxious whispers broke out all over the hall. Mr Unbar put his fingers to Darius Marriott's neck, only to cry out and instantly draw his hand away. Clenching and unclenching his fingers, he looked up and down Darius's body. From where he was sitting, Theo could see Darius Marriott's body jerk suddenly then stop, then jerk again as if he was having a fit. Shaking his hand, Mr Unbar tentatively tried again. Unclipping Darius Marriott's Lazarus suit and pulling it off, the headmaster placed his ear to the prone man's chest. He sat up and tried to take Darius's pulse again, feeling both his neck and his wrist.

"Someone phone for an ambulance," said Mr Unbar, his face grim. "Quickly. This man is dying."

2. Shock

"D'you think he's OK?" Bullet's voice was barely a whisper.

Theo shrugged. They all watched out of the classroom windows as Darius Marriott was carried away on a stretcher by two paramedics. The school gates were quite a distance from the classrooms and even further away from the assembly hall. A good width of a football pitch away at least. Theo didn't envy them, having to carry Darius Marriott all that way. As for Theo and everyone else in the hall, they'd all been bundled out of the assembly hall so quickly, Theo's head was still swimming. So much for his first thought that maybe this was some kind of joke.

"Not a very good advertisement for his own suit, is he?" said Angela.

"What's that supposed to mean?" Bullet rounded on her at once, his eyes blazing.

Theo exchanged a sigh with Ricky, then shook his head. Angela had all the subtlety of a charging rhino! Bullet and Angela made a good pair.

"I just meant..."

"Yes...?"

"I just meant that if he's had a heart attack then maybe his suit should have ... I don't know ... saved him somehow," Angela tried to explain.

"How d'you know that his Lazarus suit didn't save him?" Bullet fumed. "How d'you know that he wouldn't be dead now if it wasn't for his Lazarus suit?"

"I was only saying, Bullet. Don't bite my head off," Angela replied.

"Don't open your mouth and talk rubbish then," Bullet said in no uncertain terms.

Theo watched as Angela's face went as stiff as a board.

"Calm down, Bullet," Ricky soothed. "Angela didn't mean anything by it."

"I'm going to see if I can visit my ... visit Darius Marriott in hospital," Bullet announced.

"What on earth for?" asked Theo.

"To make sure he's all right," Bullet replied, with angry defiance. "Darius Marriott has been my hero for I don't know how long. I want to make sure he's OK."

"Why don't you just send him a card or something?"

"No, I want to see him. I can't wait any more. I have to tell him..."

Angela, Ricky and Theo waited expectantly for Bullet to finish his sentence.

"Tell him what?" Ricky prompted.

"It doesn't matter."

"Bleep! That's a lie for a start," Theo said dryly.

"Come on, Bullet," Ricky urged. "If you can't tell us, who can you tell?"

Bullet took a deep breath. He looked around uncertainly, blinking rapidly the way he always did when he was trying to make up his mind. "It's just that... Never mind. You wouldn't believe me if I told you."

"Try us," said Ricky.

"It's just that ... that's my dad they're taking to hospital," whispered Bullet.

Theo's jaw hit the floor. It was a toss up as to whose eyes were the widest open. Angela, Ricky and Theo looked at each other, then quickly back at Bullet as if they couldn't bear or didn't dare to let him out of their sight.

"Come again?" said Theo.

"Darius Marriott is my father," Bullet said, his voice firmer this time.

"Since when?" asked Theo.

"What d'you mean 'since when'? That's a funny question. He's been my dad all my life," Bullet said, a hint of impatience in his voice.

"Glad to see I'm not the only one who can ask stupid questions," Angela sniffed.

"No, I meant..." Theo shut up. He wasn't quite sure what he meant. He was in shock – complete, total and absolute!

"So will you help me see him?" Bullet asked.

"Hang on!" Ricky frowned. "When you answered his question in the assembly hall, Darius Marriott didn't seem to treat you any different to anyone else. He didn't *act* like you were his son."

"That's 'cause he doesn't *know* that I'm his son," said Bullet.

"Whoa! Whoa! You're doing another Heathrow job on me." Theo shook his head. "He's your dad and he doesn't *know* it?"

"That's right. He and my mum broke up before I was born," Bullet explained. "They used to work for a software house and Darius was my mum's boss."

"Your mum was married to Darius Marriott?" asked Theo.

"No. They used to go out together. Mum was his secretary years and years ago. Then Mum became pregnant with me and she left the company," said Bullet.

"Why?" asked Angela.

"She didn't want him to feel that he had to marry her just 'cause she was having me," Bullet replied.

"Did she tell him he was going to be a father?" asked Angela.

"No. I just said that."

"And your mum told you all this?" Ricky's frown was deepening.

"Not in so many words, but yes."

"What does that mean — not in so many words?" asked Ricky.

"Mum told me about it. She didn't actually come right out and say that Darius Marriott is my father but I put two and two together."

"Are you sure you didn't put two and two together and come up with seventeen and three-quarters?" asked Ricky.

"I'm telling you, Darius Marriott is my dad. We even look alike," Bullet insisted.

Theo had always reckoned that Bullet was the spitting image of his mum but now that he'd seen Darius Marriott up close, he and Bullet did look a little bit alike. A teensy-tiny little bit.

"Are you saying that in all these years he's never been to see you? Not once?" asked Ricky.

"No, he hasn't. But how could he? He didn't know about me. Mum never told him." Bullet shrugged. "But that doesn't matter. Because I'm going to visit him in the hospital and I'll tell him who I am and then we'll be like a real family."

Theo shifted position uncomfortably. Did Bullet really think it would be that simple? Did he really believe that all he had to do was go up to Darius Marriott, say, "Hi Dad, I'm your son!" and Darius would hold out his arms, cry out, "My son! The child I never knew I had!" and that would be that? Chewing on his bottom lip, Theo wondered if maybe he was being too cynical. Maybe he'd been around Angela for too long. Maybe Darius Marriott would welcome Bullet with wide open arms.

"I think you should take this one step at a time," Ricky said carefully. "Are you sure you've got the whole, full story from your mum?"

"Of course," Bullet frowned. "As I said, she told me some things and I worked out the rest."

"But are you sure you're right?" asked Ricky.

"What're you trying to say?" Bullet suddenly went very still.

Ricky backed off immediately. "Nothing. I just think you should be very careful of your facts, that's all."

"I am. I wouldn't have told you that Darius Marriott was my father unless I was absolutely sure." Bullet's voice was frosty.

"You've seen it on your birth certificate?" asked Angela.

"Mum says she's lost it."

"Why don't you send off for a copy, then?" Angela suggested.

Bullet stared at her. "I never thought of that."

"When are you hoping to visit your dad then?" asked Ricky.

"If not tonight, then definitely tomorrow. It's Saturday tomorrow so Mum shouldn't mind."

"Are you going to tell her what you're up to?" asked Angela.

"No. I'll visit my dad first and make sure

everything is all right and then I'll tell her," Bullet replied.

"Wait till tomorrow afternoon and then we'll all come with you," Ricky stated.

Bullet wasn't the only one who was surprised. Theo stared, then glared at Ricky. Weren't they supposed to be going to the cinema tomorrow afternoon?

"You want to come with me?" Bullet couldn't believe it.

"If that's OK? We won't get in the way – honest."

Bullet shrugged. "If you want to come along, that's fine."

"Am I coming too?" Angela asked, puzzled.

"Of course." Ricky replied before Bullet had a chance.

Theo forced the frown from his face. Ricky was up to something. That much was obvious. But what? Why was it suddenly so all-fired important that they go with Bullet when he visited his dad?

"OK. I'll try and find out from one of the teachers which hospital my dad's been taken to," said Bullet.

"And if you can't?" Theo couldn't help asking.

"Then I'll phone around tonight when I get home. I'll phone every hospital in the country if I have to," Bullet replied. "Once I find out, I'll give you a call and you three can meet me outside the appropriate hospital tomorrow afternoon at two."

"That's fine."

Their attention was called back to the window as the ambulance sped away from the school. A number of teachers stood by the school gate, talking to Mr Unbar. Soon, they turned and headed back into the school. Theo walked back to his desk with everyone else. He didn't want to be caught gawking by Mrs Daltry. Theo searched in his bag for his work book. Then he remembered that he'd left it on Mrs Daltry's table the night before. With a sigh of impatience, he got up and went to the front of the class. Yes, he was right. There it was. Theo picked it up and turned to head back to his desk. He saw that Bullet was the only one still standing at the window. And the look on Bullet's face stopped Theo cold in his tracks. No one else could see Bullet's face, only Theo – and Theo wished at once that he hadn't.

Never before had Theo seen such a look of complete and utter longing. In fact, the look on Bullet's face went far beyond longing. It was yearning and loneliness. And intense, white-hot hope. And it was directed not at anyone in the class but out of the room and out of the school. It was for the man being rushed to hospital in the ambulance. Theo felt as if he had just spied on something very personal. He just hoped that Bullet wouldn't be too disappointed if things didn't go the way he was obviously imagining they would.

3. Visiting Hours

Theo stood outside the main entrance to the local hospital, wondering for the umpteenth and three-quarters time what on earth he was doing there. It was a warm, clear, early summer afternoon. The wind wasn't nearly as biting as it had been at the beginning of the month. In fact there was a pleasant breeze blowing. And where was Theo spending the rest of his day? Stuck in a hospital, that's where! This was a wild goose chase and no mistake. And what's more, it was embarrassing. Of course Darius Marriott wasn't Bullet's dad. The whole idea was just ... silly! It was a crazy idea, mixed with more than a little wishful thinking. So what if Bullet's mum had worked for Darius Marriott years and years ago? They might even have been an item for a while. But that didn't make Darius Marriott Bullet's father. At the tap on his shoulder, Theo spun around. Angela and Ricky stood behind him.

"Where's Bullet?" asked Angela.

"At home, if he's got any sense," Theo sniffed, adding for good measure, "Which is where we should be."

"Why d'you say that?" asked Ricky.

Theo looked at him, surprised. "Isn't it obvious? This is just a waste of time."

"Darius Marriott might be Bullet's dad. Stranger things have happened," Ricky said lightly.

"D'you really believe that?" Theo stared.

"What? That stranger things have happened?"

"No. That Bullet's story is true," Theo said with impatience.

"I don't know. But..."

"But Bullet believes it's true and for now you're prepared to go along with that." Theo sighed. "This is just like you, Ricky. When

Jade said her dead dad was sending her e-mail messages you believed her, too."

"No, I believed that she believed it. And I didn't think it was impossible," Ricky contradicted. "If I remember rightly, it was you two who said that it was a trick or Jade was lying or misguided. But what about Pascoe DeMille?"

"Never mind about who or what Pascoe was," Theo interrupted. No way was he going to speculate about Pascoe DeMille again. It gave him the creeps just to think about the guy. "We're talking about Bullet and his dad. What're we going to do?"

"We're Bullet's friends so we're going to be here to help him if and when he needs us," said Ricky.

"We're nuts to get involved in the first place," Theo said.

"For once, I agree with Theo." Angela stuck in her five pence worth. "This has nothing to do with us. This is between Bullet and his so-called dad."

"Hi, everyone." Bullet's voice behind them had everyone turning around guiltily.

Chewing his bottom lip, Theo wondered just how much of their conversation Bullet had heard. Bullet looked cool and collected, far calmer than the rest of them. But Theo couldn't help wondering just how calm Bullet really felt inside. After all if Darius Marriott *was* Bullet's father, then this would be the first time Bullet spoke to him. Bullet would introduce himself as Darius Marriott's son and after that anything could happen.

"Let's go in," Bullet said.

"Is Darius Marriott definitely in this hospital?" asked Angela.

Bullet nodded. "He's in the Wellington Ward on the third floor." At Ricky's questioning look he added, "I phoned last night and again this morning just to make sure. My ... my dad's only going to be at this hospital until eight o'clock tonight. After that they're moving him to a private hospital across town and then I won't get a chance to see him. So it's now or never."

"How d'you know all this?" Angela queried.

"I told you. I phoned and asked."

"But why would they tell you?" Angela persisted. "I thought that sort of information was confidential."

"Not to family members and I'm his son," Bullet replied.

Was it Theo's imagination or was there something in Bullet's tone of voice which challenged them to contradict him?

"So what's wrong with him, then?" asked Angela.

Theo had wanted to know that too, but he wasn't sure how to frame the question. He might've guessed that Angela would come right out and ask.

"They think he might have had a heart attack but he's out of intensive care already and they reckon he'll make a full recovery," said Bullet.

"Does your mum know you're here?" Angela narrowed her eyes.

Theo shook his head. Angela got worse, she really did. Bullet glared at her. He just stared, not answering her question.

"Only asking." Angela defended herself.

Theo wondered about Angela and Bullet. At one point Angela had been mad keen on Bullet. But if she was still keen on Bullet and he was keen on her, then they had a very strange way of showing it.

"Well, we can't stay out here all day. Let's go in," Ricky said at last.

They trooped into the hospital in silence with Bullet leading the way, followed by Ricky and Angela. Theo hung behind the others. He was worried. Worried sick. He and Bullet hadn't been friends very long but they were friends now and Theo didn't want to see Bullet ... disappointed. And this whole business had DISAPPOINTMENT written over it in great big flashing capitals!

"How do we get to Wellington Ward, please?" Bullet asked the receptionist.

"Along there, turn left, take the lift up to the third floor and then along to the end of the corridor," the man behind the reception desk answered. He pointed the way, indicating the directions with his hand without once looking at them.

"Thanks," Bullet mumbled.

Without another word they all followed the receptionist's instructions. As they entered the lift, Theo thought, "If someone doesn't say something soon I'm going to ... I'm going to ... laugh or shout or bark at the top of my voice. Anything to break this silence!"

They stepped out of the lift and the strange quiet that surrounded them stepped out with them. In the distance the hospital sounds carried on as normal, but Bullet and the others walked in their own bubble of quiet concern. The corridor stretched out before them, with signs hanging down from the ceiling at regular intervals and doors and stairs leading off on both sides. They were all the way down the corridor before anyone spoke.

"Bullet, when you go in to see your dad, we'll wait outside," Ricky suggested.

"Can't we go in with him?" Angela asked, surprised.

"No, we can't," Ricky replied, getting annoyed for once. "What Bullet and his dad have to say to each other is their own private business and nothing to do with us."

Angela flushed red at Ricky's rebuke but before she could answer, they'd reached the double doors which led to Wellington Ward. Bullet took a deep breath and pushed at the doors. A huge ward spread out before them but only the patients in the first bay were visible. Immediately to their right was the ward office. Bullet marched straight up to the office and tapped smartly at the door even though it was open.

"Yes? Can I help you?" The sister in the room looked up from the report she was reading.

"I'm looking for Darius Marriott."

The sister turned to glance up at the clock on the wall behind her. She frowned. "Visiting hours don't start for another ten minutes."

"We don't mind waiting," Bullet said.

Theo couldn't understand how Bullet could be so calm. He was a nervous wreck and it wasn't even his dad.

"And you are?" The sister looked at Bullet pointedly.

"My name is Toby. Darius Marriott's my dad."

The sister glanced up at the clock again. "Oh. Well, I suppose I can make an exception just this once. But I mean just this once – d'you understand?"

"Yes, sister." Bullet grinned gratefully. "So which bed is he in?"

"Bed number fifteen. He's in a side room straight up the corridor and to your right." The sister bent her head to continue reading her report.

"Thanks." Bullet was already on his way when he spoke. Theo walked faster to catch up with Angela and Ricky. He risked a glance in their direction. It was hard to tell what they were thinking. Maybe it was just him. Maybe he was being unnecessarily pessimistic about what was about to happen.

All too soon they reached a door with the number fifteen on it. Bullet turned to look at them all, took a deep, deep breath and then pushed open the door. Darius Marriott was reading a newspaper. The doctor, a tall man as skinny as six o'clock with a very tidy moustache and dark brown hair swept back off his face, stood over Darius. He held a hypodermic syringe in one hand and in his other he held the intravenous drip line which ran into a vein in Darius Marriott's left arm. Both Darius and the doctor turned their heads at Bullet's entrance. Bullet hovered uncertainly at the door. Darius Marriott had a query on his face – nothing more. The doctor frowned, let go of the drip and slowly replaced the plastic protective cap back on the hypodermic needle. Bullet stepped into the room, still holding the door open.

"Yes? Can I help you?" asked the doctor, placing the syringe on the cabinet next to the bed.

Bullet couldn't tear his gaze away from the man in the bed. Theo's heart felt like food processor whisks on the fast setting. He couldn't have been more nervous, more apprehensive, if he was the one about to talk to his father for the first time.

"Can I help you?" The doctor repeated impatiently. He took hold of Darius's hand and slid his fingers up to his wrist to take his patient's pulse as he spoke.

"I ... I've come to see my dad." Bullet could hardly get the words out.

"You've got the wrong room," Darius Marriott said tersely. "There's no one else here. I don't share this room with anyone."

"No ... you d–don't understand..." Bullet stammered.

"I'll just take your blood pressure, Mr Marriott, and then I'll go," said the doctor. He picked up the sphygmomanometer or blood pressure machine on the table beside the patient and placed it on the bed.

"What don't I understand?" Darius Marriott asked Bullet, as the doctor unrolled the blood pressure cuff and wrapped it around his forearm.

"Mr Marriott, I'm ... I'm Toby Barker. You're my dad."

"You're ... you're not a doctor. Who are you?" Ricky's voice held fear and belligerence. "*Who are you?* What are you doing to Bullet's dad?"

Stunned, Theo turned from Ricky to the doctor. If he hadn't seen it for himself, he never would've believed it. The expression on the so-called doctor's face changed in the blink of an eye. He let go of Darius's arm and snatched up the syringe again. Bullet leapt forward as the doctor pulled the plastic cap off the needle and lunged for Darius Marriott. But Bullet was on him in an instant, knocking the syringe out of his hand. It flew across the room and hit the wall.

The bogus doctor lashed out, knocking Bullet off his feet. He snarled out a curse and leapt for the door. Theo ran over to Bullet, who lay collapsed on the floor. Ricky and Angela barred the doctor's exit. They dodged and darted around him, two terriers yapping at a giant's heels.

"Get out of my way," the man raged.

Angela and Ricky didn't answer. Nor did they take their eyes off the man. The man roared his frustration. His eyes sparked so much they could've lit matches. His hands lashed out and thrashed out as he tried to grab hold of Angela and Ricky to yank them out of his way. But they always managed just to evade his hands. With a leap, the man grabbed hold of Angela's arm but she twisted like a striking cobra and was immediately out of his grasp. Suddenly, the man charged head first for the door, like some kind of demented bull. Angela and Ricky jumped out of his way – only just in time. The door banged open and the man raced down the corridor in an instant.

"Stop him. Someone stop him," Angela yelled.

But she was too late. As the sister stepped out of her office to find out what all the commotion was about, the exit doors were already swinging shut.

"Stop him! Call the police." Angela was jumping up and down and screaming at the same time.

"Bullet? Bullet, are you OK?" Theo asked urgently.

Bullet rubbed his head as he sat up slowly. "Yeah, I'm fine. He just took me by surprise, that's all."

"Are you sure you're all right? You're not hurt?"

Bullet got to his feet. "I'm fine, I promise. But what about my dad?"

4. A Mistake

Doctor Nolan, a nurse, a woman wearing a business suit and two police officers – one in plain clothes, the other in uniform – were all crowded into Darius Marriott's room. Theo, Bullet and the others were wedged against the wall watching what was going on. Darius Marriott looked like death on a bad day. One moment he stared straight ahead profoundly shocked, the next moment he blinked like a stunned owl, the next moment his lips pursed and his eyes narrowed with fury. He didn't know what to think – or feel.

"How are you feeling now, Mr Marriott, sir?" asked the woman. She'd introduced herself as Mrs Tracer, an executive manager at the hospital. Theo wondered why she didn't wet her lips and kiss Darius Marriott's feet while she was at it. How grovelly could one woman get?

"I'm feeling fine – thanks to that boy over there." Darius Marriott looked directly at Bullet but there was no trace of a smile on his face. Bullet's head dropped, he could no longer meet his father's gaze.

Was that all the man had to say? "Thanks to that boy over there"? Theo shook his head. If he was in Darius Marriott's place, how would he feel? To be confronted with a son he'd never seen, a son he never even knew existed, and a threat to his life in the same five minutes – that would be enough to knock anyone for six. But Theo thought he would have more to say to Bullet than his dad seemed to.

"Mr Marriott, we're going to get the substance in this hypodermic syringe analysed at once," said Detective Sergeant Reid, the CID policewoman in plain clothes. "And we'll get to work on circulating your initial statements and your descriptions of the phoney doctor."

"Just what was it that made you suspect the so-called doctor in the first place?" the uniformed officer asked.

They all turned to look at Ricky. Theo had been wondering the same thing himself but in all the confusion and commotion he hadn't had the chance to ask.

"Well, first of all he was trying to take Mr Marriott's pulse on the little finger side of his wrist when everyone knows you take a pulse from the thumb side of your wrist. And then, when he tried to take Mr Marriott's blood pressure, he put the cuff around Mr Marriott's forearm instead of his upper arm," explained Ricky.

"It was very observant of you to notice. Well done!" said DS Reid.

"This is bizarre. Why would anyone want to harm me?" Darius Marriott shook his head.

"People in your position rarely get where they are without making enemies," said DS Reid. "It could be some crackpot out to make a name for himself by harming you but I'm betting the motive is a tad more mercenary."

"What d'you mean?"

"Well sir, to put it bluntly, who stands to gain by your death?"

Theo wondered at the bewildered look on Darius Marriott's face. It was as if he had never even considered the question. Moments passed and still Darius stared, too aghast to utter a word. They weren't DS Reid and Darius Marriott any more – they were Medusa and her victim!

"That's enough, officer," said Dr Nolan. "I won't have Mr Marriott any more upset than he already is."

Darius raised a hand. "It's all right, doctor. I want that fake doctor found just as much as the police do, more so in fact. If someone's trying to kill me I want them found."

"So who has a motive to get rid of you?" asked DS Reid.

"No one as far as I know. When I die, some of my money will go to various charities and some members of my staff, but the bulk of my fortune goes to the co-directors of DemTech and to my wife, Samantha."

"And where is your wife now, sir?"

"She's in New York visiting Daryl Matthewson, an old friend of hers," Darius answered.

DS Reid made a note of the New York address and phone number in her notebook. "Has your wife been informed that you're in hospital?"

"I'm not sure." Darius frowned. "My Personal Assistant Jo Fleming was here last night and again this morning. She said she's been trying to get in touch with Samantha but she's had no success."

"How long has your wife been in New York, sir?" asked the sergeant.

That's just the question I would've asked, Theo thought to himself – pleased that he was thinking along the same lines as the CID woman.

"Almost a week now."

"Does she often go abroad by herself?"

"Sometimes. It isn't always possible for us to go on holiday together. I have a very busy schedule." Darius Marriott shrugged.

He didn't look terribly bothered by that fact either. Theo couldn't imagine his mum and dad ever taking separate holidays. The thought would never occur to them. Theo regarded Darius Marriott. He took a long, hard look. And in that moment, Theo decided that he didn't like Darius Marriott very much. Correction! He didn't like him at all. There was something about him...

"Look! I really must insist that everyone leaves at once." Dr Nolan put her foot down. "Whilst Mr Marriott is in this hospital he's my responsibility. He may already have had a mild heart attack and I'm not prepared to let my patient take any more chances."

"OK, doctor. OK." DS Reid turned to the patient. "I've got your address and your preliminary statement but later on, I'll need to ask you a few more questions," she said.

"You have my card. Just make an appointment with my PA and I'll make myself available," said Darius.

Reluctantly the police, the nurse and the hospital official all left the room. Theo and the others stayed where they were. As far as Theo was concerned, he wasn't leaving until someone came right out and told him to leave. He wanted to know what was going on, more for Bullet's sake than his own, but even so! The doctor frowned in Theo's direction. Theo glanced at Bullet, Angela and Ricky. From the determined looks on their faces, they weren't about to volunteer to leave either. But just as the doctor opened her mouth to evict them, Darius said a surprising thing.

"It's OK, Doctor, I'd like them to stay."

The doctor looked like she wanted to argue, but in the end she decided against it.

"Doctor, I thought you'd ruled out the possibility of a heart attack," Darius Marriott continued, before the doctor could change her mind.

"We're still trying to work out exactly what happened. At first we thought you'd had a heart attack but your ECG readings were normal and your blood test results all came back normal as well. You have no previous history of heart attacks and no heart attack symptoms so we're at a bit of a loss to explain what happened."

"Er ... maybe there's something you

should know. I wasn't going to say anything but maybe it will help you to pin down the reason why I collapsed. And I didn't like to say in front of the police and the others," Darius said. "Just before I ... I keeled over, something happened with my suit."

"What suit?"

"My Lazarus suit," Darius Marriott provided. "It's a Lazarus waistcoat or jacket actually but that doesn't sound as good! It's been designed as a first stop medical defence system. It's meant to be worn by anyone who may need medical assistance in a hurry. It can monitor your blood pressure and pulse rate and, based on your past medical history, it can administer any necessary drugs using a hypodermic needle system. It's going to make my company a fortune."

"Never mind the advertisement! What suit are you talking about? Hold on. Is it that dark grey waistcoat thing you were wearing when you collapsed?"

Darius nodded.

"What has this suit got to do with your heart attack?" Dr Nolan frowned.

"I felt the suit give me an electric shock just before I hit the ground," Darius replied.

"An electric shock? Where?"

"Over my chest."

"But it was the shock that probably stopped your heart," the doctor stared. "Don't you realise that defibrillating a healthy heart can stop it?"

"De-what?" Theo couldn't help asking.

"Defibrillating," Ricky provided. "If your heart has stopped or it's not beating properly, they sometimes give you an electric shock over your chest to get your heart to contract then start beating properly again."

"Mr Marriott, why would your suit defibrillate your heart in the first place?" Dr Nolan asked.

"I don't know. And that's what worries me. The Lazarus suit has so many fail-safes built into it that it should never do that unless there is no other choice. The suit would never, *ever* enter defibrillation mode unless it registered that the wearer's heart had stopped beating."

"Why didn't you tell one of us this information before now?"

"Because I can't afford any adverse publicity for my project. The Lazarus suit is too important to me."

"I'd say your Lazarus suit contains a few bugs that need to be sorted out before anyone else wears it." Dr Nolan couldn't keep the anger out of her voice. "Do you realize you could've been killed? Whose stupid idea was this device of yours?"

"Mine actually." A trace of a smile flickered across Darius's face.

Dr Nolan didn't look the slightest bit embarrassed. "Well, you've done better, Mr Marriott. You've done much better."

"I've been thinking about this and the only thing I can think of is that the suit somehow malfunctioned or was tripped remotely. I was wondering if maybe, with all the gadgetry in the school hall, my invention was somehow given a false signal or a signal that confused it. If that was the case, it might've thought my heartbeat had become dangerously irregular, or had stopped altogether," Darius said, more to himself than to anyone else.

"What kind of false signal?" asked Dr Nolan. "I thought this suit of yours had all its components in the one place?"

"Yes, but it can be set up so that someone with the proper equipment can monitor your vital signs from a remote computer. The range is limited but it still works. That computer then communicates with the Lazarus suit using radio waves. If my suit somehow picked up radio waves from another source, that might've triggered the malfunction."

Every bone in Theo's body turned to mush. It felt like there were a thousand spotlights all trained on him, burning into his skin, making his blood boil in furious panic. Horrified, he turned to Bullet. He couldn't help it. Ricky and Angela were doing the same thing and Theo knew that their expressions mirrored his own. Bullet's lie detector... Was Bullet's lie detector responsible for almost killing his dad?

Theo took one look at the horror-stricken

expression on Bullet's face and immediately looked away again.

"What's the matter?" Darius Marriott wasn't slow to pick up on the atmosphere very apparent in the room.

"I..." Bullet looked around, then turned back to Darius. "I invented a lie detector and I was trying it out in the assembly hall yesterday morning."

"A lie detector? So?"

"So it uses radio waves..." Bullet's voice was little more than a murmur, but in the stunned silence of the room it was loud enough.

"You mean *you're* responsible for my suit almost killing me?" Darius straightened up, his expression thunderous.

"It was a mistake. I didn't mean it. I didn't know," Bullet pleaded.

"You tried to *kill* me." Darius Marriott was incredulous. "You stupid idiot! I ought to call the police back here to arrest you on the spot." Darius looked like he was about to leap out of the bed and throttle Bullet.

"I'm sorry..."

"Sorry? Sorry doesn't cut it. You shouldn't mess about with things you know absolutely nothing about. And then you have the nerve to tell me that cock-and-bull story about being my son. I should have you arrested for that, as well."

"Now wait just one minute," Ricky exploded.

"No, Ricky." Bullet shook his head.

"I'm not going to stand here and let him talk to one of my friends like that." Ricky refused to be quiet. "You've got a short memory, mister. All of us, including Bullet, just saved your life – or have you forgotten that? Someone was in here with a syringe and they were obviously out to get you. It was probably that same person who somehow tried to fiddle about with your Lazarus suit by remote control. You've got no right to blame Bullet when you have no proof that he had anything to do with it. What kind of father are you?"

"I'm not any kind of father." Darius snorted derisively. "That's why I wanted all of you to stay behind. I won't have that boy or any of you going around spreading lies about me. I don't know what kind of game you four think you're playing but I want to nip this in the bud before it goes any further."

"What're you talking about?" Angela scowled.

"You four have obviously cooked up this little scheme between you to get money from me or something. Let me tell you right now it's not going to work."

If Theo's mouth dropped open any further, cars would soon be driving through it! He couldn't believe his ears. Did Darius Marriott really think that they were out to extort money from him? One look at the grown-up's face and Theo had his answer.

"You must be seriously nuts!" Ricky fumed. "We wouldn't take a thing from you if we were starving hungry and you were giving away free doughnuts. We're here 'cause Bullet, I mean, Toby, told us you were his dad and we're his friends so we wanted to lend him moral support."

"If Toby or whatever his name is told you that, then he's lying."

"No, I'm not. My mum is Teresa Barker. She used to be your secretary and you two used to go out together. Mum told me so."

"Teresa Barker..." Now it was Darius's turn to look dumbfounded. "Tessa Barker is your *mother*?"

Bullet nodded. "Only her close friends call her Tessa. Everyone else calls her Teresa."

"And she told you that I was your father?"

Bullet nodded again.

Darius shook his head slowly, never taking his eyes off Bullet. "You're not my son," he said at last. "Either your mother or you is mistaken – or lying."

"Why would Mum lie about it?"

"I don't know. Maybe she's the one after my money, and she sent you to do her dirty work for her."

Bullet took a step forward, his fists clenched. "You take that back."

"I didn't mean that the way it sounded," Darius said impatiently.

Theo snorted under his breath. Darius had meant it *exactly* the way it had come out. A tense silence reigned.

"Bullet, maybe we should wait for you outside?" Ricky suggested uneasily.

Bullet immediately shook his head. "No, you're my friends. I'd like you to stay." He turned back to Darius. "Besides, I knew he'd deny it. That's why my mum left him when she found out she was pregnant with me. She knew he'd do his best to find a way to wriggle out of it. That's just the type of man he is."

"Now wait just a minute. Did your mother tell you that?"

"No. You just did," Bullet replied bitterly.

A strangely stricken look swept over Darius's face. Theo just wanted to get out of there. He'd never felt so in the way, so horribly intrusive, in his entire life.

"Look, you don't understand," Darius began.

"Oh, yes I do. I understand perfectly," said Bullet. "I'll be going now. I think I've wasted enough of your time."

Bullet turned and walked out of the door, leaving Theo and the others with no choice but to follow him.

5. If We Hadn't Turned Up

"What a slime bag!" Angela voiced her opinion the moment the door to the side room had shut behind them. "Bullet, you're better off without him."

"Angela, not now," Ricky said impatiently.

"But he is."

"Angela. Shut up," Ricky hissed.

"Excuse me." Bullet walked down the ward without another word.

"Angela, for goodness' sake! How would you feel if you were Bullet? Just remember what it was like when it was you and your brother in trouble," Ricky rounded on her.

"I didn't mean..."

"You never *mean* to say these things, but you do!" said Ricky.

Angela looked down the ward to where Bullet was walking away from them without a backward glance. "Toby, hang on. Wait!" Angela pelted down the ward after him.

"You were a bit hard on her," Theo said to Ricky. "She means well."

"Angela has to learn to think before she opens her mouth," Ricky said, not a hint of an apology in his voice. "It was bad enough for Bullet to have to listen to that man who's supposed to be his father without Angela making things worse."

They started walking down the ward.

"Ricky, what's the matter with you?" Theo asked curiously. "It's not like you to be so ... so impatient and judgmental. What's wrong?"

Ricky sighed. He looked towards the closed side room door. "I guess Darius Marriott just got to me, that's all."

"Why?" Theo asked.

"If you must know, I think ... I think I ... envy Bullet. At least his dad is here for him to find and be with. My dad's in another country and isn't the slightest bit interested in me. I guess that's why Darius Marriott got to me. He shouldn't..." Ricky got no further.

At that moment the side room door opened and Doctor Nolan stepped out. She called down the ward to Ricky and Theo. "Could you come back please? Mr Marriott would like to see you. Where're the other two?"

Theo looked down the ward corridor but Angela and Bullet were nowhere to be seen. "They've gone."

"Then you two had better step in. But you're not to upset Mr Marriott, d'you understand?" said the doctor.

"That works the other way round as well," Ricky muttered.

Theo didn't want to see Darius Marriott again. He'd had enough of that man to last him a lifetime and beyond. He looked at Ricky. If Ricky refused to go in, then so would he – but nothing doing. Ricky walked into the room. Theo had no choice but to follow.

"You wanted to see us." Ricky's tone was clipped.

"Where's ... Toby?" Darius asked.

"Your son has gone," Ricky said deliberately. "I guess he didn't want to stay where he wasn't wanted."

Darius regarded Ricky. Ricky returned his gaze without flinching.

"Do you know Toby's address?" asked Darius.

"Yeah," said Ricky.

Silence.

"Could you possibly give it to me?"

"Why?" Ricky said bluntly.

"Ricky!" Theo's voice held a warning.

"It's a perfectly reasonable question." He turned back to Darius. "Why?"

"I think I may have been a bit ... hasty. I want to sit down with Tessa and Toby and talk about this ... situation," Darius replied.

Ricky scrutinized Darius as long moments passed.

"Have you got a piece of paper and a pen?" Ricky asked at last.

Darius removed a notepad and a fancy fountain pen from his bedside cabinet. He held them out to Ricky. After a moment's hesitation, Ricky moved forward to take them. Writing quickly, Ricky soon handed the pen and pad back to Darius who immediately looked down at the pad to see what Ricky had written.

"I know where that is," Darius nodded.

"Mr Marriott, if you don't mind me asking, who d'you think that bogus doctor was?" Theo couldn't help asking.

"I have no idea." Darius's shrug of the shoulders was a little too nonchalant. "I've been wondering that myself."

"So you didn't recognize him?" Theo persisted.

"Of course not."

"What did he tell you he was doing?" asked Theo.

Darius shrugged again. "He said he had some medicine for me which had to be administered via my drip."

"Did he say what it was?"

"No and I didn't ask." Darius began to

frown. Theo knew he had to get the next question in quick!

"Your Lazarus suit, have you worn it before?"

"Yes, but not outside our research lab. We still have more tests to run before we can get them formally safety-tested."

"D'you really think they'll sell loads?" Theo asked.

"Of course. If I wasn't already a millionaire then the Lazarus suit would certainly make me one."

"And what happens if they don't sell loads?"

"What d'you mean?" Darius's frown was back with a vengeance.

"If they don't sell, will you lose a lot of money?" asked Theo.

"I don't see what..."

"I wouldn't ask if it wasn't important," Theo interjected.

"If you must know, quite a lot of my company's money, not to mention my own, is tied up in this project," said Darius. "And that's all I'm prepared to say on the subject."

"Thanks," Theo said thoughtfully.

"I can't believe I'm answering the questions of a little kid!" Incredulous, Darius shook his head, speaking more to himself than anyone else.

Little kid indeed! What a cheek! Theo glared at Darius, who didn't seem to notice.

"Are you going to be a reporter or a chat-show host when you grow up?" Darius asked Theo.

Theo shook his head, still feeling peeved at being called a little kid.

"You should seriously consider it," said Darius dryly. "You have a way of getting people to talk to you before they even realize what they're doing."

"Theo's going to be a world-famous private detective," Ricky smiled.

Theo scowled at his friend. What did Ricky think he was playing at? Theo's ambition was a secret, shared with only a few close friends.

"Is that right?" Darius raised his eyebrows. "That's very interesting."

"I'm only thinking about it. There are a lot

of things I'd like to do," Theo said defensively.

"Well, fascinating as all this might be, I think it's time you two boys left now. Mr Marriott needs to rest," Doctor Nolan said.

"We were just going anyway," said Ricky "Mr Marriott, good luck with Bullet, I mean Toby and his mum."

The only indication they got that Darius had heard was the curt nod of his head. Ricky and Theo left the room.

"Don't tell anyone else about my wanting to be a private detective." Theo rounded on Ricky at once.

"Is it such a big secret?" Ricky asked, surprised.

"Yes. I don't want the whole world to know yet – and certainly not Darius Marriott," said Theo.

"Why not?"

"I don't like him – and I don't trust him. And a detective has to trust his instincts."

"Why did you ask him all those questions?" Ricky asked.

"There's something very funny going on here," Theo replied.

"Like what?"

"I don't know what – *yet*. But I intend to find out."

"Oh dear!" Ricky sighed. "Theo, I don't think we should stick our noses into Bullet and his dad's private business, however much we might like to."

"I have no intention of doing anything of the kind. But Darius Marriott almost died at our school. And if we hadn't turned up at this hospital when we did, he might've been dead now. That needs investigating. And we're just the ones to do it."

Ricky held up his hands. "Theo, don't say it! Please don't say it!"

But, grinning, Theo said, "This is a job for the Solve-It Detective Agency!"

6. Motive

"Where's Bullet?"

Ricky and Theo were outside the hospital building now. Angela was there waiting for them. Bullet wasn't.

"He went home," Angela sighed.

"What did you say to him?" Ricky asked, eyes narrowed.

"Nothing. I didn't say anything tactless," Angela defended herself. "I apologized, that's all."

"How did he seem?" Ricky asked. "Was he all right?"

Moments passed before Angela answered. "To be honest, I don't think he was. I think, if I wasn't with him..." Angela didn't finish her sentence. She didn't have to.

"What should we do now?" Ricky asked Theo.

Theo considered. "I think the first thing we should do is find out as much about Darius Marriott, his family and his company, DemTech Industries, as we can."

"In one afternoon?" Angela said dubiously.

"We'll carry on next week if we have to," Theo decided.

"*If?* There's no if about it. It'll take us ages to find out any useful information," frowned Angela. "And finding out about DemTech and Darius Marriott wasn't exactly how I had my half-term planned. I wanted to..."

"Bullet needs us," Ricky interrupted.

Angela huffed impatiently. "OK! OK! So how exactly are we supposed to find this info?"

"The Internet, of course. Where else?" Theo smiled.

"I'll go to the library and see what I can find out," Ricky suggested.

"Good idea," Theo agreed.

"I'll go with Ricky," said Angela.

"Meanwhile I'll go home and use Mum and Dad's computer. Hopefully, it won't take me long to find out a thing or two about our friend Mr Marriott," said Theo.

"So when are we going to meet up?" asked Ricky.

"Tomorrow at three in my house – unless I phone to say otherwise. OK?" Theo replied. "See you."

The three friends split up and headed in their different directions. Theo hadn't the first clue what he was looking for. What did he hope to find? What did he know so far? Some man had tried to inject goodness only knew what into Darius's intravenous drip. The police would analyse the substance in the syringe, but how would Theo ever get the results of their analysis? That was the first problem. And then there was this so-called Lazarus suit. Had it malfunctioned on its own or did Bullet's lie detector have something to do with it? Or was there another explanation? With each step he took, Theo's lips became more compressed. There was a mystery here all right, but how would Theo get access to all the information he needed to solve it? And then there was Bullet. If Darius did turn out to be Bullet's dad, then in a way that would make what Theo had to do a lot simpler. On the other hand, it would make Bullet's life a lot more complicated. Theo had decided he didn't like Darius Marriott and nothing had happened to make him change his mind.

Theo stopped walking abruptly, making the woman who was walking behind him swerve to avoid him. Oblivious to her impatient look, Theo stood still as he thought. In the Solve-It Detective Agency's last case, Theo had made the mistake of not taking Jade's predicament seriously until it was almost too late. He didn't want that to happen again. Bullet was a mate. Theo wanted it to remain that way. And secretly, Theo couldn't help agreeing with Angela. Not having Darius Marriott for a father would be no loss as far as he was concerned. The man was a cold fish. But Theo knew he'd have to set his own feelings aside. He had to do what he could to help Bullet and the first step was to sign on to the Internet using Mum and Dad's computer.

Two hours later, Theo sat back and tilted his head in every direction to massage his tired neck muscles. He was exhausted and his eyes felt like they were perched precariously on two matchsticks. He felt like he'd read through at least a whole novel's worth of data. But at least he'd made progress. Theo looked down at the A4 sheets of paper beside his chair. He'd found at least fifteen pages of information about Darius Marriott and DemTech that was worth printing out. And nothing he'd read had changed his mind about Darius Evan Marriott. The man had been married three times, his third wife being Samantha McRae – now Samantha Marriott – who was currently in the States. Darius was forty-five and had started up DemTech Industries when he was thirty-six. DemTech stood for Darius Evan Marriott Technologies and Darius seemed to take the credit for every invention to come out of his company even though most of them were designed and researched and built by his employees. Darius was a multi-millionaire but as far as Theo could see that was the only thing he had going for him. Once again, Theo studied the organizational chart he'd drawn up for DemTech.

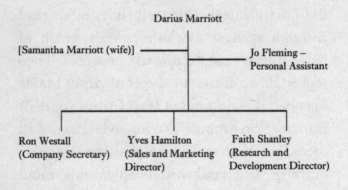

Darius Marriott

[Samantha Marriott (wife)] ———— Jo Fleming – Personal Assistant

Ron Westall (Company Secretary)

Yves Hamilton (Sales and Marketing Director)

Faith Shanley (Research and Development Director)

He had photos of Darius and all his company directors. He had their full backgrounds and CVs. Ron Westall, Yves Hamilton and Faith Shanley. In their photos, they all looked shifty as far as Theo was concerned. He had more information than he knew what to do with and yet, in a way, it felt as if he had nothing. Any of them, all of them or none of them could've been responsible for the attempt on Darius's life. With Darius out of the way, maybe one of them or all of them would take over DemTech. Maybe one of them had a mind warped enough to believe that that was a strong enough motive for *murder*. What were the usual motives for murder? Greed? Jealousy? Fear? Did any of those apply here? It was hard to know without knowing the people involved.

But Theo didn't know the directors so it was a bit pointless to speculate about their motives. He did know Darius, though. He'd met the would-be victim so he'd have to concentrate on him first. And it was strange, but Darius seemed to recover remarkably quickly from the initial shock of learning that someone was trying to kill him. But then what else was he supposed to do? It wasn't as if he could lock himself in his hospital room and refuse to come out ever again. Maybe Darius had more than an inkling as to who was trying to get rid of him? It had to be someone close to him. Someone who maybe knew about him being at their school, but who certainly knew that he was in hospital. The first thing to establish was exactly what had happened to Darius Marriott on their school stage. Was it Bullet's lie detector that had caused his dad's accident? It seemed very unlikely but Theo couldn't rule it out. Only one person would know whether or not the lie detector was involved and that was Bullet himself. Gathering up the DemTech data off the floor, Theo ran out of the room and downstairs.

"Mum, can I go round to Bullet's house?"

"What? Now?" Mum glanced down at her watch. "It's almost six o'clock."

"It's really important," Theo pleaded. "And I'll be back in an hour, I promise."

"I don't know, Theo. It's a bit late to go visiting. Can't you leave it until tomorrow?" asked Mum.

"No, I can't. I really can't. It's very important, Mum."

Theo's mum regarded him with a frown. A huge grin spread over Theo's face. "Thanks, Mum."

"I didn't say yes," Theo's mum protested.

"Thanks, Mum." Theo was already in the hall and heading for the door.

"An hour." Theo's mum stressed as she followed him. "I want you back in an hour and you're to go straight to Bullet's house and then straight home again. D'you understand?"

The front door was open. "No problem. See you later."

"Theo..."

Theo didn't wait to hear any more. He needed to see Bullet. Bullet was the key to this whole mystery.

7. The Unexpected Guest

"Hi, Miss Barker. Is Bullet in?"

"Hello, Theo."

Theo took a good look at Bullet's mum. It was as if he was seeing her for the first time. Usually she received the briefest of glances to make sure she hadn't sprouted two heads or something and then Theo swept past her on his way to find Bullet. But now that he knew a bit more about her, he was more interested. She was a lot younger than his mum. Theo reckoned she was in her early thirties at the very most. Theo's mum was Jurassic, in her forties and climbing. Or was the word deteriorating! Bullet's mum had short hair parted on one side and swept back off her face and dark brown, twinkling eyes. And she always wore leggings or jeans. Theo had never seen her in a skirt or a dress.

Bullet's mum turned with a frown to look at the clock hanging on the hall wall. "Is something wrong?"

"Oh no. I just wanted a quick word, that's all," Theo assured her.

"Hhmm. Well, you'll have company. Ricky and Angela just arrived saying the same thing." Bullet's mum missed Theo's start of surprise as she turned to take another quick look at the clock. "Come on in, then."

Theo stepped into the house and Bullet's mum shut the door behind him. "They're all in the living-room. I wish I knew why you all look so serious."

Bullet's mum's voice was mildly curious, inviting Theo to confide in her, but Theo didn't answer. He walked into the living-room. Bullet was sitting at his computer – naturally! – whilst Angela and Ricky sat on the sofa. And it didn't take a clairvoyant to realize that there was a very frosty atmosphere in the room. Nodding his hello, Theo sat down next to Ricky. Bullet's mum looked around the room.

"Would any of you like something to eat or drink?" she asked.

"No, thank you."

"No, thanks."

Theo shook his head.

"I ... er ... I have some things to get on with in the ... er ... upstairs, so I'll leave you all to it," Bullet's mum said.

Even when Bullet's mum had shut the living-room door behind her, still no one spoke. And then, without warning, Bullet sprang out of his chair.

"So why are you here, Theo? To tell me how you've been sticking your nose into my private business as well?" Bullet raged.

"Pardon?"

"You heard me. These two," Bullet waved a dismissive hand at Angela and Ricky, "these two have been telling me how you all decided to stick your noses in where they're not wanted."

"We're only trying to help you," Theo

protested. "We thought as we all have a week off, we could..."

"Who asked for your help?" Bullet blazed. "I certainly didn't. And as for helping me, are you sure having another stupid case for your rotten detective agency didn't come into it somewhere?"

"Theo never even mentioned our detective agency," Angela stormed back at Bullet.

Theo bent his head, guiltily. He *had* been thinking about the Solve-It Detective Agency, it was just that Angela hadn't been present at the time – but that wasn't all there was to it.

"Bullet, you're not being fair. We're just trying to help," said Ricky quietly.

"Help with what? I don't need your help. I told my dad that I'm his son and he wasn't interested. That's it. End of story."

"But what about that bogus doctor in his hospital room? Don't you want to find out what that was all about?" Theo couldn't help asking.

"And what about when he keeled over on our school stage yesterday morning?" said

Ricky. "I don't know about you, but I want to know what's going on."

"Why?" asked Bullet.

His question momentarily threw all three of them.

"That's a strange question," Angela frowned. "Someone's out to get your dad. Aren't you interested in finding out who and why?"

"No," Bullet answered immediately.

Angela opened her mouth to respond but Ricky placed a restraining hand on her arm and shook his head. Theo was barely aware of the front door bell ringing outside the room. He was so wrapped up in what was going on in Bullet's living-room, he was barely aware of anything else.

"Are you really not interested?" Ricky asked.

"That's right."

"Don't you even want to know if it was your lie detector yesterday that made Darius's Lazarus suit malfunction?" Theo couldn't believe Bullet could be that blasé about what had happened.

"Now that I've had a chance to think about it and test it out again, I know it *wasn't* my lie detector," Bullet replied.

"How d'you know?" Theo asked.

"Because it's not possible. I..." Bullet got no further.

At that moment the door opened and to Theo's stunned amazement, in walked Bullet's mum followed by Darius Marriott. A collective gasp echoed in the room as they all regarded the unexpected guest. And Theo wasn't the only one who looked as if he'd just been slapped around both cheeks with a dead trout. Bullet's mum looked like she'd just seen a ghost. Looking at her, Theo tried to determine whether Darius's arrival was a nice or nasty surprise but her face was now shuttered off, an expressionless mask.

"I see I'm interrupting," Darius said easily.

"No, not at all. Bullet's friends were just leaving," Bullet's mum said meaningfully.

Theo, Ricky and Angela immediately stood up.

"Yes, that's right, Mr Marriott. We were

just leaving," said Ricky. He turned to Bullet. "Don't worry, Bullet. We won't be troubling you with this matter any more if you don't want us to."

"Where're you going?" Bullet asked.

"We've got to go home," Ricky said. "Besides..." Ricky turned to look at Darius Marriott. He didn't need to say anything else.

"Could you stay, please?" Bullet asked.

Theo looked from Ricky and Angela to Darius and then back to Bullet. He wondered who Bullet was talking to.

"Toby, I don't think..." his mum began.

"It's OK, Mum. My friends know that he's my father." Bullet's voice was lemon-bitter as he turned to face his dad. "And they know just what he thinks of the idea, too."

"They know *what*?" Bullet's mum asked sharply. "How could you tell them or anyone else such a thing?"

"Why not? It's true, isn't it?"

"This isn't something I care to discuss in front of all and sundry," snapped Bullet's mum. "And Toby, I'll thank you not to broadcast this family's private business."

"If I can't tell my close friends then who can I tell?" Bullet replied.

It was funny the way things worked. A few minutes ago, Bullet was on the verge of throwing them out and never speaking to any of them again. And now here he was, declaring that Theo and the others were his close friends. Theo could feel his face begin to burn as he looked around the room. He was embarrassed – he couldn't help it. He felt totally out of place, like a fifth wheel or a third leg.

"Tessa, I would like to talk to you and Toby in private, if you don't mind," said Darius.

"Bullet, we do have to be going now," Ricky interjected when Bullet would have protested further. "We'll see you tomorrow or Monday. Just call if you need anything – OK?"

Reluctantly, Bullet nodded. As they left the room, Theo looked up at Darius. Why was he here? What was he thinking? What was he *after*? Oh, to be a fly on the wall! Theo trooped out after the others but not before he'd given Darius a long, hard look and made sure that Darius knew he was being scrutinized. If Darius did anything, anything at all to upset Bullet, then Theo would find some way to pay him back.

'You just see if I don't,' he thought, hoping that his thoughts were clearly readable on his face. He couldn't help it, but he still didn't like Darius Marriott and what's more he didn't trust him, either. Not one little bit.

8. Where There's A Will

"So he didn't phone you either?" Ricky asked.

"Nope," Theo replied, disappointed. "I was hoping he would but ... no."

"Not one call all last week?"

"Not a peep. Not a beep." Theo shook his head. "Is he here yet?"

"No. He wasn't outside. And he's not in the computer room either," Ricky said, amazed.

Monday morning – and every school morning come to that – always found Bullet in the school's computer room, fiddling with one of his programs. But not today.

Angela sighed. "I called round to see

him last Sunday, Tuesday and again yesterday."

Ricky and Theo stared at her.

"You're joking!"

"You never!"

Angela raised her eyebrows. "Of course I did. What was I meant to do? Sit at home and wonder all week?"

"That's what we did," Ricky pointed out.

"Yeah, well, I couldn't wait that long. I wanted to make sure that Bullet was all right."

"You are so nosy!" Theo told her with a mixture of admiration and irritation.

"The nosiest," Ricky agreed. "So how was he? Was he OK?"

"I'm not going to tell you," Angela sniffed.

Ricky and Theo looked at each other, puzzled. "What d'you mean you're not going to tell us?"

"You two are just hypocrites!" said Angela. "You sit there condemning me for being nosy and then, with the next breath, you ask me to share the results of my nosiness! You two need to get together and make up your minds what you really want."

Theo had to admit that Angela had a point. "OK, sorry. Now tell us what happened."

"Not until you admit that you like me to be nosy 'cause it means I do your dirty work for you."

"We admit it. We admit it!" Ricky said, exasperated. "Now, what happened?"

"Bullet and his mum weren't in – at least, not any of the times I called round," Angela shrugged. "And I phoned them every evening at seven and there was no answer."

"I wonder where they were all week." Ricky voiced the thought in all their minds at that moment.

The classroom door opened and as if on cue, in walked Bullet. Bullet was usually one of the last ones to come into the classroom. He worked up until the last possible moment on the computers in the school terminal room. But when he did come into class, usually he made a beeline for Theo and the others. But not today. With just a faint smile in their direction, Bullet walked straight over to his chair and sat down at his table. Angela, Theo and Ricky exchanged a glance, wondering what was going on. Theo led the way as they walked across the classroom.

"Hi, Bullet. How goes it?"

Bullet shrugged. "Fine."

"Everything all right?" asked Ricky.

"Yeah, fine."

"Did you have a good week?"

"Yeah, great."

Was that all he had to say to them? Theo tried and failed not to get annoyed.

"So what did Darius want when he came round to your house that Saturday, then?" asked Angela.

Bless her! Theo had to bite his lip to stop himself from laughing outright.

"If you must know, Angela, he came to apologize," said Bullet. "He said that not only am I his son but that he's glad I am. We sat and talked for a long while and then he took us out to dinner."

"Why the sudden change of heart?" Theo couldn't help asking.

"I think my announcement that I was his

son was just as much a shock to him as it was to me when I found out. It never occurred to me that he would be fazed by the news," Bullet replied.

Theo remained silent. It all sounded very reasonable. Very plausible. And yet... And yet. Darius had been more than adamant that he was not Bullet's dad. And now he'd done a whole one hundred and eighty, welcoming Bullet with open arms. What was he up to? Theo sighed inwardly. Maybe the man wasn't up to anything. Maybe he really had changed his mind. Theo sighed again. He'd have to watch this cynical, pessimistic attitude that he seemed to be developing!

"I'm glad for you," Theo said sincerely.

Bullet grinned. "Thanks."

"And where were you yesterday and all last week?" said Angela.

"Pardon?" blinked Bullet.

"Where were you? I knocked for you a couple of times and I phoned you every night last week," said Angela.

"If you must know, Mum went to stay with my aunt whilst I spent the week with my dad

– and I'm getting more than a little tired of you, Angela."

"Huh?"

"Since when did I have to report to you?"

"I wasn't expecting you to report to me. I was just concerned."

"Don't you mean 'prying'?" Bullet asked scornfully. "My dad said I should be careful about my so-called friends now. He said a lot of people will only want to be my friend so that they can get to him through me."

Theo's mouth dropped open so fast, he nearly dislocated his jaw – and he wasn't the only one. This seemed to be a continuation of the conversation they'd had in Bullet's living-room over a week ago, only it had taken a bizarre and much more hurtful twist.

"We're not your friends because of your dad," Angela said with indignation.

"And why would we want to get to your dad? I don't even like the man," Theo fumed.

"Bullet, you've got a nerve. We were your friends long before your dad arrived on the scene," Ricky reminded him furiously.

"No, you weren't. I was just a nerd who

happened to know his way around a computer. That's the only reason you talked to me in the first place," Bullet said.

"That's not true. I mean, that's not the whole story," Theo amended at Bullet's sceptical glance. "OK, that might've been why we first started talking to you but we all considered you our friend after that."

"You obviously didn't feel the same way," Ricky said quietly.

Theo recognized that tone at once. Bullet had gone too far. Even Bullet seemed to recognize that maybe he'd said too much.

"I didn't mean that the way it came out. But my dad said that now he's changed his will, I have to choose my friends very carefully," Bullet tried to explain.

"Now he's done *what*?" asked Theo, the rest of Bullet's sentence lost on him.

Bullet looked around, then beckoned them closer. "I'm only telling you three this because ... because I know that you're my friends really," Bullet whispered. "But my dad changed his will last Thursday. His lawyer visited him whilst I was at his penthouse flat. He's left some of his money to his staff and some close friends, but he's left his company, DemTech Industries, to *me*."

No one said a word at that. Not even Angela. They all stared goggle-eyed at Bullet. It didn't even cross Theo's mind that this was a wind-up. Bullet was too earnest, too serious.

"But I want you all to promise that you won't tell another living soul. I promised Dad I wouldn't tell anyone, so you've got to promise, too. OK?"

"We promise." Theo raised his right hand. Angela and Ricky did the same.

"Why is he leaving you his company?" Theo asked when his voice had fully returned.

"'Cause I'm his son, of course!" Bullet replied, eyebrows raised.

"Yes, I know. But you've only known the man for five minutes. He can't have changed his will already," said Theo.

"Well, he has."

"Why?"

"What d'you mean?"

Theo grew more and more puzzled by the second. "I mean, what's his rush? If he really has changed his will, why did he change it so quickly?"

"I'm his son."

"Yes, but... Ricky, what d'you think?" Theo appealed to his friend to back him up. Surely he wasn't the only one who thought this whole thing was bizarre. Ricky shrugged and said nothing. Theo frowned at him, trying to decipher his expression but Ricky's face was a mask. Theo turned to Angela. He felt sure that her expression mirrored his own.

"But why isn't he leaving the company to his wife, Samantha? What does she get?" Theo continued.

Bullet frowned. "Dad never mentioned her. I guess she'll get his money and I'll get the company. Or maybe they have one of those special agreements that rich people make when they don't want to lose all their money. One of those pre-nuptial agreements?"

"Twit!" Ricky laughed. "Rich people make pre-nuptial agreements before they get married. It's so they can protect their money if they ever get divorced. I've never heard of an agreement to cut out the other person if one of you dies."

"Just because Dad never mentioned it, doesn't mean he didn't leave her anything," Bullet defended rigorously. "Besides, maybe Dad's set it up so that she already has all the money she needs."

"From what I've seen, rich people never have all the money they need. They never have enough." Theo shook his head. "But congratulations, Bullet. That's brilliant news. Good for you."

Bullet smiled. "To be honest, I don't even care about the money. I'd always planned to be a famous inventor and make my own money. What I can't get over is saying the word 'Dad'! My dad! I still can't quite get used to it. It's wonderful. All these years without a dad and suddenly I've got one – and it's Darius Marriott."

Ricky lowered his head.

"What did your mum say about all this?" asked Theo.

"She was furious with me at first. She never told me the name of her boss all those years ago, so I had to do some tracking down. All she said was that she and a man she'd worked with had been very much in love and she became pregnant and decided to leave without telling him."

"So how did you pin it down to Darius Marriott being your dad?" asked Theo.

"Mum stopped working when she was pregnant with me and she only started working again when I was seven. I found some old pay-slips she'd hidden away and then used the Internet to track down the software company they'd both worked at before Dad started DemTech. Then I wrote to them and asked if I could retrieve some of their archive information. I told them it was for a project I was doing for school," Bullet explained.

"And they let you do that?" Theo asked, surprised.

"I told them I was just interested in how their personnel department worked and how they had set about computerizing their records. They invited me in for a morning to see their computer system."

"They didn't let you on their computer, did they?" Ricky stared.

Bullet started to grin. "Well, Mrs Brosser, the Personnel Manager, was called away for ten minutes..."

"And she left you in front of her computer?" Ricky winced.

Bullet's grin grew even broader.

"What a mug!" Ricky laughed.

"I pretended I didn't know much about computers whilst she was showing me around so she probably thought it was perfectly safe to leave me." Even Bullet's eyebrows wriggled about in smug pride now.

Ricky used his elbow to nudge Theo in the ribs before nodding in Angela's direction. Angela was staring at Bullet, a strange expression on her face.

"Angela, you're very quiet," said Ricky.

Angela never took her eyes off Bullet. The hurt in her eyes was being overtaken by a hard, sombre look that Theo hadn't seen in a long, long time. "I don't want to be accused of sticking my nose in where it's not wanted."

"Angela, I..."

"Excuse me." Angela didn't wait for Bullet to finish. She turned abruptly and walked off.

"I didn't mean to upset her," Bullet mumbled.

"Yes, you did," Ricky contradicted. "Angela liked you and stuck up for you long before anyone else gave you a chance and you were really mean to her."

"Yes, Saint Ricky. Sorry, Saint Ricky." Bullet bowed with sarcasm. "Who d'you think you are?"

"I know who I am. And that's not someone who thinks he can switch his friends on and off like a tap whenever it suits him," Ricky snapped.

"I don't do that."

"That's exactly what you're doing. A moment ago you said you were telling us about your dad's will 'cause we're your friends, but now you're acting like a cow pat again," Ricky told him straight.

"Listen, I don't need you or anyone else in this rotten school. My dad says he's going to pay for me to go to a private school so I don't have to mix with people like you any more."

People like you! Theo opened his mouth to tell Bullet exactly where he could stuff his private school but Ricky got in first.

"Bullet, you needn't worry about 'people like us' polluting your breathing air any longer. See you around." Ricky walked off without a backward glance.

Theo scowled, wanting to tell Bullet exactly what he thought of him but he was so angry he knew if he opened his mouth, his words would fall out in an inarticulate, furious jumble. He took a deep breath, and another and another.

"You've had a dad for exactly ten days and money for less than a week and look at how it's changed you," Theo said slowly and quietly. "If you ask me, you were better off without either of them."

"But no one did ask you. So you can push off along with Ricky."

"I don't mind if I do," Theo told him.

"Oh, and as for my birthday party two weeks on Saturday, don't bother coming. I'm sure you don't want us riffraff inflicting our lower-class germs and bacteria on you."

Theo turned to walk away. Bullet called out after him, "I wasn't going to come anyway. My dad's taking me out."

Theo refused to turn back to dignify Bullet's boast with a response. As far as Theo was concerned, the Solve-It Detective Agency was now back down to three people. Jade, who was meant to be part of the agency, had moved with her mum up to Manchester to be closer to the rest of their family. Theo and the others had been really sorry to see her go, but as for Bullet... His was definitely a case of good riddance to bad rubbish. Theo couldn't believe the change that had come over Bullet. Bullet didn't seem to know what he wanted. He talked about Theo and Ricky and Angela being his friends and yet in the next breath he insulted them with a nastiness that took Theo's breath away.

Was that really what money did for you? If it was, then Theo wasn't sure that he wanted to be rich. No, he took that back! He did want to be rich, but he'd handle it a lot better than Bullet. He wouldn't be moronic enough to think that he was better than all his friends just because he had more money than them. He wouldn't dream of insulting his friends in the way that Bullet had just done. It was as if Bullet reckoned they didn't have any feelings.

Theo couldn't help sighing as he sat down next to Ricky. There was no doubt about it. Sudden money seemed to do strange things to a lot of people's minds. And so many rich people seemed to be so miserable. Mind you, Theo would rather be miserable with money than without! It was better to be miserable in comfort. Theo turned his head. Bullet was watching him and Ricky, with a strange, almost forlorn, expression on his face. An expression which disappeared almost as soon as Theo looked at him, to be replaced by something that Theo had no trouble interpreting. Theo gritted his teeth. If Bullet didn't stop looking at him like Theo was something nasty he'd just trodden in, Theo was going to march across the room and tell

Bullet one or two things about himself. Just who did he think he was? It'd be a long time before Theo forgot what Bullet had just said. He wasn't going to forgive him that easily either. Giving him the filthiest look he could, Theo turned his head away, utter contempt in his every gesture. He risked a quick glance at Bullet to see if he had made his feelings for his former friend clear. Bullet purposely avoided Theo's eyes. Theo gave a slight smile of bitter satisfaction. So much for his ex-good-friend Bullet Barker. If Theo never spoke to him again, it would be too soon.

9. Reckoning

"Why did you drag me down here to the car park?" The man looked around anxiously. "We shouldn't be seen together like this."

"You're the one who told me not to talk to you in the office. You said Darius probably had the place bugged," the woman reminded him.

"I wouldn't put it past him." The man looked around the empty car park again. "So what's so important that it couldn't wait until tonight?"

The woman sighed and shook her head. "I think we should call a halt. We should quit while we're behind."

"No way. No one suspects us. We're OK."

"But he's changed his will," the woman replied, anguished. She began to pace up and down, rubbing her hands together in an agitated mime of washing them clean.

"Yes, I know."

"Don't you understand? He's changed his will. That changes everything."

"No, it doesn't. It just means we have to get rid of the boy before we deal with Darius."

The woman froze in her tracks. "You can't be serious. Getting Darius out of the way is one thing. But getting rid of his son is something else again."

"Darling, we have to. We haven't got any choice." The man took the woman by the arms and hugged her tight. "We can't stop now. We just can't."

The woman pulled out of his grasp. Bitterly, she said. "Your plan to use the Lazarus suit to get rid of Darius failed. He survived and we were moronic enough not to let things be. We should've quit then but no, you had to hire someone to try again – and they got caught."

"It wasn't Jake's fault. He said those kids came in just as he..."

"I don't want to hear it." The woman turned her head away.

"Darling, listen to me. We can't stop now. We're both up to our necks in this – and we both have too much to lose."

"So what do we do now?"

"I don't know. Jake's panicking and he's bleating to get paid. He wasn't supposed to get any more until ... until Darius was no longer a problem. But now that the police have his description, he wants to disappear as soon as possible – and of course that takes money."

"We haven't got it. You tell him that."

"I already have," the man said with impatience. "But he doesn't want to hear it. I'm afraid he might try something ... foolish."

"Where did you find this guy?"

"That hardly matters now. The point is, we're stuck with him."

"Look! I just want to forget about the whole thing," the woman said firmly. "We should just keep our heads down."

"What about Jake? He wants money."

"Well, he can't have it."

"He could make a great deal of trouble for us."

The woman shook her head. "Not without making a great deal for himself too. He's hardly likely to complain to the police, is he?"

"He might do. And he knows who I am," said the man.

"He doesn't know me." The woman managed her first slight smile since the meeting had begun. "And I can provide you with an alibi for the time when he tried to pull that little stunt at the hospital."

"I don't think that would work. I was in a bar around the corner from the hospital waiting for him. I'm sure someone there could recognize me," the man argued.

"How could you be so stupid?"

"I didn't expect him to tell me he'd failed," the man snapped.

It was a long time before either of them

spoke. The woman said at last, "It's only a matter of time before Darius finds out about you and me and then he'll put two and two together and he'll come up with the right answer."

"That's why we need to act quickly."

Long moments passed as the allies regarded each other. "OK then. I'll carry on with this – because I love you," the woman said sadly. She drew herself up to her full height. "If we're going to get rid of the boy, it should be soon."

"Good!" The man drew a sigh of relief. "I knew you wouldn't let me down. Don't worry. I'll tell Jake that he still has some work to do."

10. Look Out!

"**D**'you two think this is all my fault?"
"Huh?" Ricky looked at Angela, surprised. "What on earth are you talking about?"

Angela shrugged. "The way Bullet turned on the three of us. I know you two think I'm really tactless and nosy as well, but I didn't mean to..."

"Angela, stop talking rubbish," Ricky dismissed. "Bullet's behaviour had nothing to do with you being tactless. Besides, he should be used to that by now!"

School was over for another day and the three friends were walking home. It was a wet and windy Thursday afternoon and as far as

Theo was concerned, the weather suited his mood. For four whole days, none of them had exchanged a single word with Bullet. Deep down, Theo had to admit that he actually missed his former friend. He hated the icy silence that had descended between them. And what was worse, neither Angela nor Ricky had mentioned Bullet since the big bust-up. But since Monday, whenever the three of them were together, they'd all lapse into strange silences where it was obvious that they were all thinking about the same thing.

With a sigh, Theo looked up at the sky. It was peculiar weather for the end of May. Until that morning the last week had been unseasonably hot and breezeless. Theo remembered reading somewhere that hot, breezeless weather made people a lot more irritable and short-tempered. If that was the case, then it would explain a lot as far as Bullet was concerned. Maybe now that it was raining and the air was cooler, things would get back to normal.

"It's just that, I can't help thinking that I

somehow made things worse between all of us, not better." It was plain to see that Angela was brooding about the events of the last few days.

"Forget it, Angela. Bullet just thinks he's too good to walk on the same planet as us, that's all," Theo sniffed.

Ricky shook his head. "I don't know. I don't think so. I think it's more than that."

"What d'you mean?" asked Angela.

"It's just that I've now had a couple of days to cool off and think about it. And d'you know something? When Bullet was saying all those things to us, it was as if it wasn't him saying them at all. It was as if someone else – maybe that Darius Marriott bloke – was talking through him," said Ricky thoughtfully.

Theo raised his eyebrows. "That's a bit fanciful, isn't it? I reckon it was just Bullet the wazzock talking!"

Ricky shrugged, but said nothing.

"I don't know what's going on," Angela said, bemused. "Bullet and I used to be such good friends. At one time I actually fanc... I mean, I liked him a lot!" Angela amended, her cheeks flaming red. "But now, it's like every time I open my mouth I annoy him."

"Maybe we're not giving him a chance," suggested Ricky. "Bullet's got a lot to deal with right now. Maybe we should all just..."

"Ricky! Theo! Just a minute, Angela!"

They all turned to see Bullet come puffing up behind them. He had to cross a broad road to get to them and he gave the briefest of glances to his left and right before charging across. Without warning, a dark car seemed to rev from a standstill to an instant eighty kilometres an hour and it came racing towards Bullet, who had now reached the middle of the road. Theo was the first to see it.

"NO!" Theo yelled a warning.

"Bullet, look out!"

Bullet turned his head and saw the car racing towards him. Shock froze him to the tarmac. Ricky leapt forward – but Angela beat him to it. She dashed into the middle of the road, just as the car was almost upon Bullet and shoved him out of the way. Angela tried to dive after him, but she wasn't so lucky. The side of the car hit her and Angela was knocked into the air. And in that moment, Theo's heart stopped beating. As Angela hit the ground, Theo could hear the THWACK-CRACK from where he was standing. And when Angela hit the ground, she stayed perfectly still, her eyes closed. The car roared up to the next corner, its brakes shrieking as it raced around it. And now Theo's heart was racing. In a shocked daze, Theo looked up the road but it was too late. The car had gone. Ricky was already squatting down at Angela's side. Icy cold, Theo walked slowly to the middle of the road. Already a crowd was beginning to gather and the cry was going up for an ambulance and the police.

"Is she...? Is she...?" Bullet whispered.

Angela lay crumpled up on her side, her leg bent at a very peculiar angle beneath her. And the road beneath her head glistened red with a thin trail of blood running from her forehead.

"She's still breathing – but she's in a bad way," Ricky said grimly.

A short, broad man with a crop of dark hair squatted down next to Ricky. "Let's try and make her more comfortable..."

"NO!" Ricky shouted. "No. You mustn't move her. We have to wait for the paramedics to arrive. If you move her you could make things worse, not better."

"He's right. You shouldn't move accident victims," a woman from the ever-growing crowd joined in.

"Did anyone see the car that did this?" asked the short, broad man.

"It raced off around the corner," another man from the crowd volunteered.

"Did anyone get the licence plate number?" someone else asked.

Stricken, Theo looked up the road in the direction the car had driven off. He'd been so shocked, so stunned by what had happened he couldn't even remember his own name when it was all going on, much less the licence plate of the car. He tried to think back. What colour was the car? Dark blue. Navy blue. What make was it? He didn't know. He wasn't sure. If only he'd been more together. Then he could've noted all the details for the police. He was useless. Some detective he was. Angela had been knocked over in front of him and he couldn't say whether it was a man or woman driving and all he could remember was that it was a medium-sized, navy blue car. Even Ricky had been quicker off the mark than he had been.

"She ... she pushed me out of the way..." Bullet's tremulous voice was just one of many. If Theo hadn't been looking at him at the time, he would never have caught what Bullet said. "She pushed me out of the way. She saved my life."

All around, the crowd were asking each other what had happened, what they should do, where was the driver of the car that had hit the girl. The question buzzed round and around Theo's head like hungry bluebottles.

In the distance an ambulance siren could be heard, getting closer and closer.

"Theo, take Bullet to your house. And don't leave until I get there." Ricky's sudden command was harshly said.

"I... What about the police and the ambulance people and..."

"Never mind all that. I'll tell them what happened. Just take Bullet and go," Ricky ordered.

Theo took another look at Ricky's stony expression and grabbed Bullet by the arm. "Come on, let's go." Theo pulled him away from the crowd.

"I want to stay here." Bullet tried to pull his arm out of Theo's grasp.

"No, you can't. Come on. You're coming home with me."

"No way. I want to stay with Angela. I want to make sure..."

"Bullet, don't be so stupid. You've got to come to my house where it's safe," Theo hissed at him. Part of the fury in his voice was directed at himself although Bullet had no way of knowing that. "The driver of that car was after *you*. He was trying to *kill* you and if it hadn't been for Angela he would've succeeded. We've got to get you somewhere safe. Now come on."

11. More Questions Than Answers

"Who would want to kill me?"

Sourly passing up the chance to tell Bullet that anyone who'd ever met him might feel that way, Theo kept silent. Bullet was sitting at Theo's work table in his bedroom, his expression still glazed and dazed. Theo glowered at Bullet, but Bullet didn't seem to notice. Theo told himself that he was being unfair. What had happened wasn't Bullet's fault any more than it was Angela's, but after everything that had happened over the last few days, Theo found himself resenting the fact that it was Angela being whisked off to hospital in Bullet's place. It wasn't that he wanted to see Bullet injured or hurt in any way, but it wasn't *fair*.

Theo's scowl deepened as he felt guilty for the direction in which his thoughts were taking him. Theo decided he'd better keep his mouth shut. Rage bubbled in him like lava in a volcano. He knew he was just waiting for any excuse to lash out and the closest person to hand at the moment was Bullet.

"I don't understand. Who would want to kill *me*?" Bullet whispered again.

Theo forced his lips together tight, tight, tight. He turned away from Bullet. If he heard that one more time...

"I mean, who would want to...?

"Oh, for goodness' sake!" Theo exploded. "Don't be so stupid. You spent Monday morning boasting about your dad leaving you everything in his will. Well, you may be ecstatic about it but it's obvious you and your dad have cheesed someone else off!"

The horrified expression on Bullet's face as he turned to face Theo had him feeling even more rotten.

"I'm sorry," Theo said grudgingly. "I shouldn't have blurted it out like that but Bullet, start working those brain cells. You may know a lot about circuits and computers and microchips and that, but you don't know much about people – especially adults."

"You really think my life is in danger? That it was deliberate?" Theo could barely hear Bullet's voice now.

"I've been thinking about that." Theo forced his voice to be calm and collected. "The car came straight at you. It started up when you began to cross the road. So yes, I do think it was deliberate."

Bullet stared at Theo but didn't answer.

"I didn't get it at first either. When Ricky told me to take you straight to my house it took a couple of seconds for the reason why to click into place," Theo admitted.

"You're faster on the uptake than me." Bullet's lips were a thin slash across his face as he spoke. "Seems I've been getting a lot of things wrong recently."

"What d'you mean?"

"Never mind."

Theo didn't push it. He didn't envy Bullet one little bit. What was the point of having millions coming your way when you couldn't even cross the street – literally. Theo's thoughts slid back to Angela. He sat down on his bed and sighed.

"I wish Ricky would hurry up and get here. I wish I knew how Angela is doing."

"Why did Angela do it?" At Theo's questioning look, Bullet said, "Why did Angela save my life after all the vicious things I said to her?"

"Maybe she reckoned it was worth saving? Or maybe she just acted on the spur of the moment and didn't realize what she was doing," Theo provided with a certain malicious relish.

"If she dies..."

"Don't say that. Don't even think that," Theo stormed. "Angela will get better – and soon. I just know it."

"You know more than me then."

"Bullet, I swear if you don't shut up I'm going to chuck you out."

"Sorry."

"Anyway, why were you chasing after us?" asked Theo.

"Pardon?"

"Before the accident. You were running after us. What was that all about?"

"Oh yeah!" Bullet turned away from Theo. "I... I wanted to catch all of you together. I wanted to apologize for all the things I'd said."

"And you reckoned an apology would make up for it," Theo said scornfully.

"No. But it's all I have," Bullet said quietly. He suddenly covered his face with his hands. "I'm so confused. Dad told me that I have to ... to think and act like his son now, but..." Bullet broke off, the look on his face expressing clearly that he felt he'd said too much. He looked at Theo defiantly, daring him to comment. Theo turned away, determined to keep his mouth shut.

They sat in silence, apart from each other, not even facing in the same direction. The seconds turned into long, painful minutes and still no one spoke. Just when Theo thought he was going to explode with the silence, the door burst open, making both Bullet and Theo jump.

"Ricky!" Bullet leapt to his feet.

"Your mum sent me straight up," Ricky told Theo.

"How's Angela? Is she OK? Is she badly hurt?" Bullet asked anxiously.

"She woke up as the ambulance arrived. She's broken her leg and has a concussion but the paramedics will know more when they get her to hospital," Ricky told them.

"I thought you were going with Angela to the hospital," Theo said.

"I wanted to, but the ambulance woman told me that I couldn't because I'm not a relative. She said I could visit Angela once she was comfortable in hospital," said Ricky.

"Did Angela mention me at all?" asked Bullet.

Ricky nodded. "She asked if you were OK. I told her you didn't have a scratch on you."

Ricky and Theo stood facing Bullet. The tension in the room was a tangible thing, charged like summer lightning.

"Go on. Why don't you just come right out

and say it? It should've been me, not Angela in hospital now."

"Don't be ridiculous. Why would I wish it was you instead of her? The thought never even crossed my mind," Ricky said angrily.

Theo hung his head. He knew he couldn't say the same thing.

"Don't lie. I know you reckon this is all my fault."

"Look Bullet, when you're ready to talk sense and stop feeling sorry for yourself, let us know." And with that, Ricky deliberately turned his back on Bullet.

"Are you sure Angela's going to be OK?" Theo asked. "I've been sitting here worried sick."

"I can only tell you what I was told." Ricky shook his head.

"I want to visit her as soon as possible," said Theo.

Ricky nodded his head in agreement. "OK, we've got to find out who was driving the car that tried to knock down Bullet. It's a shame we can't see a copy of Darius Marriott's wills – both new and old. That would give us a list of suspects to start from."

"Why do we need to see the old will?" Theo frowned.

"Because of what happened the Friday before half term," said Ricky. At Theo's blank look, he continued. "I think Mr Marriott's heart attack – if that's what it was – was not as spontaneous as it looked."

"Why?" asked Bullet.

Ricky completely ignored him.

"Why? Because of the bogus doctor?" asked Theo.

"Mainly that. But also this Lazarus suit. If it can be activated by remote control but only at a limited range, how do we know that there wasn't someone nearby who set it off, hoping it would kill him? Then Mr Marriott's own invention would've been blamed for his death. If I wanted to get rid of him, then that's how I would do it."

"D'you think that's what happened?" asked Bullet.

"Hhmm! Did you hear something?" Ricky asked Theo lightly.

Theo shrugged. It was hard work pretending Bullet wasn't in the room, but this was where they found out once and for all where Bullet stood. If he left the room and left the house, then that would be that and Theo and Ricky would be on their own.

"Did Mr Marriott come to our school with anyone else?" Ricky asked. "That might be worth finding out. And we need to know exactly how close another person has to be to send remote messages to the Lazarus suit."

"But what about Bullet's lie detector?" said Theo.

"What about it?" asked Ricky.

"I thought that had something to do with Mr Marriott's Lazarus suit being activated," said Theo.

"Certainly, we can't rule it out. But in light of what happened at the hospital, it'd be one ginormous coincidence if Bullet's lie detector made Mr Marriott's suit malfunction and then someone used that opportunity to try and bump him off."

"But coincidences do happen," Theo pointed out.

Ricky nodded in reluctant acknowledgement. "It'd be nice to know exactly how this lie detector works and how the Lazarus suit works, to see if one could have really set off the other."

"I can tell you that," said Bullet eagerly. "I can show you the lie detector and Dad's Lazarus suit."

"But our first aim should be to find out exactly what's in this new will," Ricky mused.

"Stop ignoring me. I'm sorry – OK. I'm sorry." Bullet pulled Ricky around to face him. "And I can probably get you a copy of the will."

"So you're with us now, are you?" Ricky asked coolly.

"Yes, I am." Bullet replied at once.

"How can you get the will?" Theo asked.

"The lawyer brought it round for Dad to sign yesterday," said Bullet. "Dad keeps all his important papers and documents in the safe in his study, so I might be able to get hold of it for you to see. Or maybe I could just copy it on to Dad's computer using his scanner and then print it out."

"How d'you know where your dad's likely to keep the new will?" asked Ricky.

"Well, he kept the old will in his safe so I don't see why he wouldn't keep the new one there too," Bullet replied

"You learnt all this in a couple of weeks?" Theo asked, impressed.

"Dad showed me his safe when he showed Mum and me around his flat two weeks ago," said Bullet.

"He lives in a flat?" Theo was surprised.

"A penthouse flat. He has flats in New York, Paris, Rome and Sydney too."

Theo wasn't surprised!

"What about the safe combination?" asked Ricky.

"The safe's on an electronic timer," said Bullet.

"So?"

"So I have a device at home that can handle that," Bullet smiled.

"Don't tell me. Let me guess. A device you made yourself?" said Theo.

"Natch!" Bullet agreed with no attempt at modesty.

"Pardon?"

"Naturally. Natch," Bullet explained.

Theo and Bullet regarded each other, slowly smiling. And the harsh words of the last couple of days were, if not forgotten, then on their way to being forgiven.

"What's our plan of action?" asked Ricky.

"Mum and I are going round to Dad's for dinner tonight. I'll see if I can get hold of a copy of Dad's will then," said Bullet.

"How is your mum with all this?" Theo couldn't help asking.

"She ... she wasn't too happy, but she says she's getting more used to the situation now," Bullet admitted. "When she first found out what I'd done, she hit the stratosphere. When she'd finally cooled off, we sat down and talked for four hours straight. She told me I should've told her what I was doing. But how could I? I didn't want to hurt her feelings. I didn't want her to think I was looking for something better."

"Is that what she thought?" Ricky stared.

"Until I put her straight," Bullet sighed. "She didn't think she'd given me enough information to work it out and she reckons I should never have gone to Dad and told him who I was without speaking to her first."

"Well, it's done now," said Theo.

"Any chance that she and your dad...?"

"No. None at all. Mum made that very clear," said Bullet. "Besides Dad's married now, anyway."

They sat in a moment's silence, contemplating just how complicated Bullet's life had suddenly become. With all the weird things happening to him, it was no wonder he was acting very peculiarly!

"OK then. You're going to try and get hold of a copy of your dad's will for us to see. Just don't get into trouble over it," said Theo.

"Don't get caught, then you won't get into trouble," Ricky said bluntly.

Theo sighed deeply. "The trouble is, we have far more questions than answers at the moment."

"But not for long," Ricky replied without hesitation.

"If someone is trying to get me out of the way, I hope we get the answer to all our questions before they succeed," said Bullet.

Only the hiccupy catch in Bullet's voice belied the evenness of his words. He wasn't as collected about this as he was trying to make out. Theo didn't expect him to be either.

"Bullet, Ricky and I will come with you if you want to go to the police. In fact maybe that's what we should do, before you get hurt."

"I've got no proof." Bullet shook his head.

"We're your proof," Theo insisted. "We'll tell the police how that car came straight for you. And Angela's your proof. She's in hospital, isn't she?"

"Yes, but the driver might have been drunk or just not looking where he or she was going," Bullet argued.

"Then why didn't the driver stop?" asked Theo.

"I don't know, all right? Some drivers just don't stop when they've been in an accident. It happens all the time," said Bullet.

"Bullet, you need to think very seriously about this," Theo stated. "I'm not waiting for someone to put me, you or any of us in the hospital – or worse – to satisfy your need for concrete and absolute proof. It seems to me that you're waiting to get proof over our dead bodies!"

"Don't you dare say that," Bullet shouted. "All I have to do is think about Angela and what happened to go icy-cold inside. It should've been me and it could've been a lot worse. Don't you think I don't know that? I'm not *stupid*."

"Calm down, Bullet. Theo never said you were," Ricky soothed.

No, but there was no doubt about it. Hanging around Bullet was getting to be a dangerous occupation. The driver of the car hadn't been after Angela. He or she had been after Bullet. And look what had happened. Theo sat up with a start. He'd just thought of something else. Something that was making his heart jump.

"You ... you don't think the driver will try to get to Angela?" Theo whispered.

From the stunned look on Bullet's and Ricky's faces, it was obvious they hadn't considered the possibility either.

"You don't think the driver will think that Angela looked into the car and can identify him or her?" Theo continued.

"No! No." Ricky's protest at the idea burst out of him. "Angela was too busy pushing Bullet out of the way to see anything or anyone else."

"Yes, but does the driver know that?" Theo persisted.

"Of course. I'm sure Angela never took her eyes off Bullet," Ricky said firmly.

Theo nodded slowly, clenching his fists. He had to get a grip! If he wasn't careful he'd be jumping at shadows.

"It's just that, if there's even a chance that the driver might try to get to Angela in the same way he or she tried to get to Mr Marriott, then we really should go straight to the police," said Theo.

"It won't happen," said Bullet.

"You're sure of that?"

"Yes. The driver wanted ... wants me.

Angela has nothing to do with this. Besides, I won't let anything else happen to Angela – or any of you."

"Like you can do anything about it," Theo dismissed.

"I'm the one the driver wants. So can you just shut up about it, please?" Bullet yelled.

"No, we can't," Ricky joined in. "If something were to happen to you too, we'd never forgive ourselves. If you go to the police, they'll be able to protect you."

"I'm not going to the police and that's all there is to it," Bullet said fiercely.

"Why not?"

"I have my reasons."

"Care to share them?" Theo asked after a brief pause.

"No."

"We could go without you?" Ricky suggested, steel in his voice.

"I'd deny everything," Bullet shot back at once. "I'd tell them you're making it all up."

Theo opened his mouth to argue, only to snap it shut again. What was the point? Bullet had obviously made up his mind.

What did he hope to achieve with his ostrich act? That wouldn't make his dilemma go away. There were no two ways about it. Someone was after Bullet and if they didn't find out who and stop them, Bullet was as good as dead.

12. Shadows And Shadows

"Theo, Ricky's on the phone."

"Mmmm! Urgmmm!" Theo pulled up the duvet further around his neck and allowed himself to drift off again.

"Theo! Ricky said it was urgent."

Reluctantly, Theo opened his eyes. He glanced at the clock radio on the floor beside his bed. Then he groaned. "Mum, it's six-thirty in the morning."

"Why don't you tell Ricky that? He's your friend, not mine." Mum stood in the doorway, wearing her dressing-gown. And she didn't look too pleased either.

Theo dragged himself out of bed and rubbed his eyes. So this was what half-past six on a Monday morning looked like! As far as he was concerned, if he never saw it again it would be too soon. Stumbling to his feet, Theo made his sleepy way downstairs.

"You had better be at death's door," Theo said the moment the phone receiver was to his ear.

"Good morning to you too!"

"It's not the morning. It's the middle of the night," Theo grumbled. "What d'you want?"

"Charming! I need you to meet me at the corner opposite the newsagent's at seven-fifteen," said Ricky.

"You must be joking. I'm going back to bed."

"No, you can't. Bullet's at his dad's flat. He wants us to meet him there before school."

"Why?"

"He wouldn't say. He just said it was very important."

"But it's so early," Theo protested.

"You're not saying anything that I haven't already said to Bullet. But he said it was urgent so I said we'd be there."

"Couldn't you go by yourself?" Theo said hopefully. His bed was calling to him and Theo was finding it hard to resist.

"Theo, don't be so lazy," Ricky said impatiently. "Get out of bed and I'll see you in forty-five minutes."

And with that Ricky put down the phone. Theo sighed, forcing his eyes to stay open. A shower would wake him up, but the problem was coming up with a plausible explanation for why he wanted to leave the house so early.

"Mum, Dad!" Theo called as he headed back up the stairs. "I've got to go round to Ricky's. He's panicking about our test today."

Theo's mum appeared bleary-eyed from her bedroom. Behind her, Theo could hear his dad snoring.

"You're going round to Ricky's before school?" Theo's mum couldn't believe her ears. She pinched her arm. "I'm obviously still asleep. It takes a cannon to wake you up and an earthquake to get you out of bed."

"Well, I'm not happy about it, but Ricky needs my help." Theo yawned.

"Helping Ricky revise is all very well, but

make sure you're not late for school." Theo's mum wagged her finger.

"Yes, Mum. I'm off for a shower."

"Would you like some bacon and eggs on toast" Theo's mum asked.

"Oh, yes please." Great! He was going to get breakfast before he left the house.

"So would I!" Theo's mum nodded and headed straight back into her bedroom.

"Very funny, Mum," Theo called after her, but her bedroom door was already closing. Calling himself all kinds of a fool for falling for his mum's strange sense of humour yet again, Theo had his shower and got dressed. Grabbing a cold chicken drumstick from the fridge, Theo set off to meet Ricky.

"This had better be as important as Bullet thinks it is," Theo fumed.

"Shush! Keep your voice down." Ricky nodded his head in the direction of the suited man who sat two seats in front of them.

"Why would he be listening to our conversation?" Theo whispered.

"He got on at the same stop as us and the

bus is practically empty, yet he chose to come and sit back here with us."

"So?"

"So I'm just keeping my eye on him, that's all," Ricky whispered tersely.

Theo looked at the back of the man who sat before them. He had light brown hair and wore glasses but that was all Theo could make out.

"It's just a man on his way to work," said Theo.

"Probably." Ricky shrugged. "But it doesn't hurt to be ... cautious. Anyway this is our stop."

"I still can't believe I'm doing this," Theo grumbled as he and Ricky got off the bus. "I must need my head examined."

"Stop moaning," Ricky groaned. "You're giving me a headache."

Ricky and Theo started walking past some of the cleanest, swishest-looking buildings Theo had ever seen in his life. He and Ricky exchanged a look.

"How the other half do live!" Theo said dryly.

"How the lucky five percent do live!" Ricky amended.

"So where's this flat then?" asked Theo.

"It's not a flat. It's an apartment," Ricky corrected loftily.

"Where is it then?" Theo looked behind, wondering if perhaps it was back the other way. But what was that? Was it his imagination or had someone ducked into an alleyway a little further down the road? He turned to Ricky, wondering if his friend had seen the same thing, but Ricky was busy looking for the number of the building before him. Frowning, Theo looked down the road again. He was certain someone had ducked out of sight when he turned. Theo walked slowly back the way he'd come. Back towards the alleyway.

"Theo, where're you going? It's this way," Ricky beckoned.

"I just want to check something out," Theo called back. He ran the rest of the way to the alleyway and looked down it. Neither its smell nor its appearance were particularly inviting. It was strewn with boxes and rubbish and other things that looked entirely less savoury. And it was dark – towering buildings rising like giants on either side of it. There was no one there and, as far as Theo could see, no one would want to go down there, either. And yet, somewhere in there amongst the shadows... Theo shivered. The whole alleyway had turned into a malevolent presence.

"Theo, are you coming or what?" Ricky called impatiently.

Taking one last look, Theo turned and walked back to Ricky. They carried on walking together.

Ricky started reading off the numbers of the buildings. "Fifty-nine to sixty-nine. It must be the next building along."

Theo turned sharply. A man walking behind stopped to look at one of the buildings.

"Ricky, I think we're being followed," said Theo.

Ricky turned around. "What? Are you sure?"

"No," Theo admitted. "But I'm sure that

man was hiding in the shadows of the alleyway and now he's pretending to be looking at that building."

"Wait a minute. Isn't that the man who was sitting two seats in front of us?" asked Ricky.

Theo stared. "Is it?"

They both turned all the way around to look at the man they suspected of following them. The man took a piece of paper out of his pocket and looked down at it before looking back up at the building. He turned around and walked in the opposite direction away from them.

"Maybe we're both a little jittery." Ricky shrugged.

"And maybe we aren't," Theo countered.

The front of the next building consisted almost entirely of marble and glass. Behind a huge desk against one wall sat two uniformed security guards. The foyer of the building consisted of huge plants and glass and mirrors. Theo had never seen anything like it. Theo and Ricky looked for a door bell for Darius Marriott's apartment but there was none. Instead there was a bell to press for

Reception. Raising his eyebrows, Ricky pressed it. Theo could see the two security guards watching them. Then he heard a loud click. Ricky pulled at the door and they entered.

"Can I help you?" asked the older of the security guards.

"We're here to see Bullet, I mean Toby Barker. His dad is Darius Marriott. He asked us to meet him here."

"Just a moment." The security guard picked up one of the two phones on the desk in front of him and looked Theo straight in the eye. "Hello, Mr Marriott. I have two children down here who say they're here to see your son... Yes, sir." The guard turned back to Theo and Ricky. "And your names are?"

"Theo Mosley. And this is Ricky Burridge," Theo provided.

The security guard repeated the information over the phone. "Yes, sir... No, sir... Very good, sir."

Three bags full, sir! Theo thought sourly. What was it about Darius Marriott that had all the grown-ups around him bowing and scraping? The man's farts were probably just as smelly as everyone else's!

"Take the lift over there and press the button marked P," ordered the security guard.

Without another word, Theo and Ricky did as they were told. Only when the lift doors had shut behind them did they speak.

"Have you ever seen anything like this?" Theo asked. "This lift has got a better carpet in it than we've got in our whole house! And this building is something else. Mr Marriott must be rolling in it."

"He probably has a room in his apartment full of money and he goes in there every day and just jumps up and down and rolls about in it," Ricky sniffed.

"Ah! But is he happy?" Theo asked seriously.

He and Ricky looked at each other. "Yes!" they said in unison.

The lift doors opened. Bullet and his dad stood outside an open door beyond which

Theo and Ricky saw the biggest living-room they'd ever seen. Darius wore a royal blue shirt, a golden yellow tie and a navy blue suit which fitted so well it had to have been made for him.

"Hello, Mr Marriott."

"Good morning, Mr Marriott."

"Morning. I can't stop. Help yourself to whatever." Darius rushed past them into the lift.

"Bye, Dad."

Darius just had time to wave before the lift doors closed.

"In a hurry, was he?" said Ricky, dryly. "So Bullet, I'm bursting to know what was so all-fired urgent that you had to drag us out of bed at six o'clock in the morning."

"How come you're here and not at home?" asked Theo.

"I spent the weekend with my dad. It's OK. Mum said I could."

"You're round here a lot these days, aren't you?" Ricky said thoughtfully.

"Is your mum here too?" Theo asked.

Bullet shook his head. "She wouldn't come

even though Dad invited her. But she said she understands that me and Dad want to get to know each other better. I sometimes wish..."

"Wish what?" Theo prompted when Bullet shut up.

"It's just that it would be so perfect if Mum and Dad... Well, there's no use talking about it. It's not going to happen." Bullet shrugged.

Theo and Ricky followed Bullet into the penthouse. Only when they were inside the apartment, could they appreciate the living-room's true size and splendour.

"Wow! This isn't a living-room. Clear all the furniture out of the way and two professional teams could play a decent game of football." Theo whistled appreciatively.

One wall of the living-room was entirely made of glass and the view was spectacular. They could see most of the town and into the country beyond. The sky was a clear, morning blue and in the distance Theo could see a plane banking. He walked over to the window and looked out over the town, wondering if he'd be able to make out his house from here.

"Where's your dad gone, then?" asked Ricky.

"He had to leave for an emergency meeting," said Bullet.

"So where's the fire?" Theo turned to ask.

"I wanted to show you around and show you some things before his housekeeper arrives. We're only going to be alone for about another twenty minutes, half an hour at the most," Bullet explained.

"I thought you were going to scan your dad's will into his computer and get a print-out." Theo frowned.

"I don't want to risk it. I don't want to risk taking anything out of this apartment that I shouldn't. Dad told me that he's got security devices all over the place."

"What kind of security devices?" Theo and Ricky looked around anxiously.

"I can't see anything," Ricky said slowly, still checking the corners of the vast room.

"That's the thing. I've looked everywhere and I can't see the first hint of a security device. Dad's security is brilliant." Bullet grinned.

"So how are we going to see the will?" Theo asked. "I don't want to do anything that'll have shutters banging down and lights flashing and will get Tweedledee and Tweedledum at the desk downstairs up here."

"I think we're OK as long as we don't try to take anything out past the front door," Bullet said.

"You don't sound too sure," said Ricky.

"I'm not," Bullet admitted.

"What explanation did you give your dad for inviting us round here?" asked Theo.

"I asked him if you could come round before school to help me revise for our test today," Bullet explained.

"And your dad was OK with that?"

Bullet smiled. "He believed me. Why shouldn't he? Besides, I think he thought I just wanted to show off his apartment to you."

"Can't think why!" Theo said wryly, looking around again.

"Come on. This way. We'd better get cracking before the housekeeper arrives. The safe is in Dad's den."

Suppressing the urge to make a sarky remark, Theo followed behind Bullet who led the way to one of the rooms on the right, leading off the living-room. The den consisted of a large mahogany table upon which sat a PC screen, printer, scanner, modem and loud speakers. The floor was polished parquet wood with a huge rug in the centre of the room. The rug was a revelation in itself. Its pattern consisted of white peacocks displaying their snow white tail feathers, whilst between them and around the edges smaller midnight-blue and turquoise peacocks tried to peck at them. And the peacocks were so beautifully embroidered, Theo expected them to burst out of the rug and take wing at any second. Around the walls there was shelf after shelf of books. Theo walked around, curious about the sort of things a millionaire liked to read. It was all non-fiction. And most of the books were about military whatevers.

Military machines. Military strategy. Military tactics. Military doodahs – past, present and future. Theo wrinkled up his nose. How boring. Apart from the large table with all the computer equipment on and under it, there were two huge black leather chairs beneath each window and one wall of the den was covered in paintings, most of which Theo recognized as famous ones done by people like Monet and Van Gogh. Theo's mum and dad liked paintings – especially Impressionist paintings – but they bought the posters and then framed them. Theo was in no doubt at all that every painting in this room was the real thing. He couldn't help wondering, did Darius Marriott own those paintings because he liked them and they gave him pleasure, or did he own them so that he could say he owned them?

"Dad calls that his picture wall." Bullet smiled.

"It's a great room," Ricky said.

Theo didn't think so. In spite of the morning light streaming through the window, the room was cold and dark and uninviting.

"Dad's safe is under the rug." Bullet headed straight for it. "Help me roll it back."

They all helped to roll back the rug until more than half of the floor was exposed. Pulling the rug out of the way, Theo and Ricky went back to Bullet to check out the contraption in the floor. And there it was – a rectangular door, a little smaller than the cupboard doors in Theo's kitchen at home. It was made of a silver-coloured metal. In the middle of the door was a keypad. Theo had expected a round tumbler device with numbers all around it like they always showed on telly. Bullet took a small device out of his pocket, like a thick compass with two antennae sticking out of it. Also attached to it were two earpieces on a longish cable, like the earpieces sometimes supplied with a portable tape or CD player.

"That's your safe cracker, is it?" Theo asked.

Bullet nodded, putting the earpieces in his ears.

"So how does it work then?"

"It sends a phased series of pulses to the opening mechanism microchip and analyses differential micro delays in response times so that..."

"Nope, forget it. It's another Heathrow job already." Theo waved away the explanation which had already lost him.

"When you try a random number for the combination, the computer takes a different amount of time to say 'no' based on how wrong the number is. By timing the delay you can home in on the right number pretty quickly."

"Hang on." Theo frowned. "With a keypad you could have any number of numbers and in any order. I don't see how your device is going to help in this instance."

"I know all the numbers except the last one and I know the last one consists of three digits," said Bullet. "So all I have to do is find that last three-digit number before Mrs Frayn the housekeeper arrives."

"Go on then. Do your stuff," said Ricky, glancing down at his watch. "But hurry up.

We still have to get to school after all this. I'll wait by the door and warn you if anyone comes in."

Ten minutes later the safe still wasn't open.

"Bullet, we're running out of time," Theo said anxiously.

"I know. I know. I'm doing my best," Bullet replied.

Another seven minutes passed before the safe door finally clicked open.

"At last!" Ricky breathed a sigh of relief. He went back to the centre of the room to get a better look. Hanging down on suspended rods were hanging files, each containing papers and more papers.

"I think Dad's will is in here somewhere." Bullet started hunting through the hanging files.

"What's the rest of this stuff?" Theo couldn't help asking.

"Research notes on new inventions, notes on the Lazarus suit, that kind of thing. Plus details of most of Dad's bank accounts around the world."

"He's got more than one account?" asked Ricky.

"Of course," said Bullet, as if it was the most natural thing in the world. "Ah, here it is. Dad's will."

Ricky and Theo gathered in closer, eager to see what it contained. They all read in silence for a couple of minutes.

"All that legal jargon is a bit hard going but as far as I can see, you get everything apart from a few thousands scattered around to some of his staff and some of his favourite charities," Theo said at last.

"Yes, but have you seen this bit?" Ricky turned to the third page of the will. "If Bullet dies before Mr Marriott then the terms of the old will apply."

"Bullet, what were the terms of the old will, d'you know?"

"Yeah, Dad told me. As far as Dad's DemTech shares are concerned, Ron would've inherited twenty-five percent, Yves and Faith would've got eleven percent each and Jo was due to get four percent."

Theo's expression grew pained as he did

some less than rapid mental totting up. "Hang on. That doesn't add up to one hundred, that only adds up to fifty-one."

"Dad's only got fifty-one percent of the company's stock. At the moment, Ron has fifteen percent, Faith and Yves have thirteen percent and Jo has eight percent of the company."

"But – have I got this right? – according to the old will, if your dad's shares were split between the four of them, none of them would've had outright control of DemTech. Ron would've inherited the most, giving him – my head hurts! – forty percent of the company, but that's not enough to run things," Theo pointed out.

"Maybe Dad didn't want any one of them running the company. Or maybe it was a device to make them all work together? I don't know." Bullet shrugged.

"Your dad told you an awful lot about himself and his company in a very short space of time," Ricky said speculatively.

"We've had great talks." Bullet beamed. "We had a lot of catching up to do."

"But why would he tell you so much about his wills and the DemTech set-up and the rest?" Ricky persisted.

"'Cause I'm his son, of course," Bullet said, surprised that Ricky even had to ask.

"It's just that..."

"What was that?" Bullet's head turned immediately towards the door. "Quick! Give me the will."

Bullet snatched the will out of Ricky's hands and stuffed it back into its hanging file before slamming the door shut.

"The rug! Quick! The rug!" Bullet hissed.

Theo rolled and Ricky leapt in the rug's direction. Bullet sprang out of the way as Ricky and Theo rolled it out like pushing a barrel. They straightened up the rug just as the door opened.

"Hello, Mrs Frayn..." Bullet's voice trailed off as they all stared at the woman who entered the den.

If this was Mrs Frayn then she was like no other housekeeper Theo had ever seen. She wore a bright red evening dress and a midnight-black mink coat. And something told Theo that it wasn't fake fur.

"Well now. Who might you three be?" the woman asked. "No, don't tell me. Let me guess." She pointed straight at Bullet. "You're Darius's long-lost son. Correct?"

Bullet gulped and nodded.

The woman scrutinized Bullet as if he was under a microscope. It wasn't that Theo and Ricky were forgotten. It was as if they weren't even there. They were of no more interest than passing ants on the pavement.

"Toby Barker..." The women breathed Bullet's name, her tone dripping with the smile on her face although, for the life of him, Theo couldn't see what was so amusing. The woman looked around, before turning back to Bullet.

"Tell me," she said at last. "How much would it take to make you and your mother disappear?"

13. Mrs Marriott

"I don't understand." Bullet's voice came out in a squeak.

"You're obviously after my husband's money but I'm back now. And I'm going to make sure you don't get one brown penny from Darius's will. So I'll ask you again, how much will it take for you and your mother to make yourselves scarce?"

"I don't want Dad's money," Bullet replied indignantly. "That's not what this is about at all."

"No?" Mrs Marriott crossed the room, overpoweringly sweet perfume wafting behind her. It made Theo want to sneeze. "Then exactly what is this all about?"

"I just wanted to see Dad. I wanted ... I want to be with him," said Bullet.

"There's no room for you in his life, or mine," said Mrs Marriott.

"That's not what Dad said," Bullet told her.

"But then he wouldn't. Darius always leaves it to me to do all his dirty work for him." Mrs Marriott's laugh was a tinkling bell. No one could deny that she was very beautiful. She had shoulder length auburn hair and deep grey eyes framed by the longest eyelashes that Theo had ever seen. Some people might've looked silly wearing an evening dress at this time in the morning, but she didn't.

"Did my dad tell you to get rid of me?" Bullet's voice was barely above a whisper.

"Of course not. But he will do," said Samantha. "At the moment, you're a new experience for him. He's never played at being a daddy before. He'll soon get bored."

Never before had Theo witnessed such a display of vindictive spite. This woman was a real piece of work. She reminded Theo of a swaying, spitting cobra, mesmerizingly dangerous. He longed to open his mouth to defend his friend but he was only too aware that it was none of his business.

"Dad isn't like that." Bullet tried to defend himself.

"No?" Mrs Marriott shrugged out of her coat and trailed it behind her on her way to the door. "I've known him for a lot longer than you. Allow me to know my own husband."

"Dad is kind and generous and he loves me," Bullet shouted at her.

Mrs Marriott laughed like a drain at that. "That's what you think? Darius loves no one but himself. You'd do well to remember that – then you won't be too disappointed."

Bullet clamped his lips together, not trusting himself to say another word.

"What are you three boys doing in here anyway?" Mrs Marriott suddenly turned her gaze on Ricky and Theo. She looked slowly around the room then down at the rug.

"Ah! Have you been at Darius's safe? I hope you broke in and tore up that ridiculous will. I know the combination number if you're having trouble," Mrs Marriott smiled.

"We don't even know where Mr Marriott's safe is," Theo tried.

"Of course not," Mrs Marriott said in mock empathy.

"What makes you think we were looking at Mr Marriott's safe?" Ricky asked carefully.

"Darius insists that the biggest white peacock, there in the middle, always faces due north – which is that way." Mrs Marriott pointed towards the picture wall. "That peacock always has his beak directly facing the Degas in the middle of the wall."

No one spoke.

"I'd turn the rug around before the housekeeper or my husband comes home if I were you three." Samantha Marriott turned and headed out the door, calling back over her shoulder, "I'll be seeing you."

"Not if I see you first," Bullet muttered under his breath.

Samantha turned immediately. "But that's where you're wrong, Toby. You and I will be seeing a great deal of each other. I'm back now. And don't you forget it." And Samantha swept out of the room, quietly closing the door behind her.

"Whew! I feel like I've just stepped out of a tumble dryer," said Ricky.

And Theo knew exactly what he meant. "Come on. Let's change this rug around before anyone else notices that we've shifted it."

As they all helped to turn it back to its correct position, Ricky put into words what everyone else was thinking, "Why did she warn us? I mean, what was in it for her?"

"Maybe she's going to tell Dad that I was investigating his safe?" Bullet ventured.

"But now she has no proof – unless of course she was lying about the way the rug lies," Theo said slowly.

"I hate to say this, 'cause I didn't like her at all, but I don't think she was lying somehow," Ricky said slowly. "I think she hates your guts, Bullet, but I don't think she was lying to you."

Theo considered. "No, I don't think so either."

"So what do we do now?" Ricky asked.

"Let's get out of here." Bullet headed for the door. "Besides, there's something else I wanted to show both of you."

"What?"

"Dad's suit of life as he calls it. His Lazarus suit." Bullet led the way out of the den and into another room off the main living-room.

"What's this room?" asked Ricky, pointing to the room Bullet indicated.

"It's my bedroom when I'm here," Bullet explained. "It's one of the guest rooms."

He led the way into his room and closed the door. The Lazarus suit lay on his bed.

"Why did you want to show us this?" asked Theo.

"'Cause I want you two to be my witnesses," said Bullet. "I've tested it and tested it backwards, forwards and sideways and my lie detector doesn't set it off."

"It's not exactly the same conditions," Theo ventured. "No one was wearing it."

"I was," Bullet stated.

"What?" Ricky and Theo spoke in horrified unison.

"You nutter! It might've killed you," Ricky ranted.

"No way. I know Dad's invention works. Besides, I tested it range-wise, height-wise, frequency-wise, amount of light-wise and every other wise I could think of. My lie detector doesn't activate this suit. In fact the only thing my lie detector does is switch the suit off. It doesn't do anything else."

"This thing has an on/off switch?" Theo said, confused.

"No, not really, but it has a number of electronic components. If any of those components are activated, then using my lie detector nearby stops them from working. In effect it switches all the electronic components off."

"Including the defib... defibrillation bit." Theo tried to remember the word.

"Including that." Bullet nodded.

"So how exactly does it work?" Theo reached out a tentative hand towards the suit.

"Just as Dad said. It's designed to be ultra-thin so that it can be worn under a shirt and a proper suit. The high collar would be hidden by a shirt with a proper collar and it has a mechanism in it to take the pulse in your neck. There's a cardiac massage unit, a defibrillation device – but that's only ever used as a last resort – it can take your blood pressure and it can administer injections like insulin in times of emergency."

Theo broke out his notepad.

"What're you doing?" asked Bullet.

"I'm taking notes. I want to draw this thing just so I don't forget what all its bits and pieces do. It might be important."

"Just remember that the details of this suit are strictly confidential," Bullet said anxiously.

Theo nodded and carried on drawing.

"Do you think your dad's Lazarus suit will take off?" Ricky asked.

"I don't know," Bullet replied. "All the really successful inventions involve things that have mass-market appeal so that lots and lots of people will buy them. But apart from presidents and prime ministers and famous film stars and maybe royalty, I don't really see who else would buy it. It's going to be hideously expensive to buy and cost even more money to maintain, monitor and operate."

"If the price is really high, your dad's company will still make a huge profit even if they only sell a few thousand world-wide, won't it?" asked Ricky.

Bullet shrugged doubtfully. "That's the theory."

"I see you have better business sense than my husband." Samantha Marriott had appeared from nowhere to stand in the doorway. Bullet jumped and he wasn't the only one. Where had she appeared from? How long had she been standing in the doorway? Theo could've sworn he'd shut the door behind him as he entered the room.

Samantha Marriott reminded him of a snake in more ways than one.

"I only came in here to say don't you three have school to go to or something?" asked Mrs Marriott. "Not that it's any skin off my nose if you go or not. I just don't want to get blamed for not mentioning it."

"We were just leaving ... Mrs Marriott." Bullet stumbled over her name.

A slight smile played over Samantha's lips. "Toby, as you're obviously uncomfortable saying my name, you can call me ... Mrs Marriott."

No doubt she thought she was being hilariously funny.

"Enjoy yourselves, sprogs. I'm off for a hot bath and a cold glass of champagne." Mrs Marriott swept out of the room, leaving the door wide open.

"What an old cow!" Ricky breathed.

"She was right about the time though," Theo said, glancing down at his watch. "We'd better get a move on or we're going to be late."

"Theo, you go on ahead. I want to talk to Ricky about something," said Bullet.

"Then I'll wait too," Theo began.

"No, you go on ahead. We'll meet you at school," Bullet said firmly.

Theo stared from Bullet to Ricky and back

again. He tried – and failed – not to feel hurt by his exclusion. What had he done? Why were they shutting him out? Confused, he didn't move.

"I'll show you to the door," said Bullet.

"Don't bother. I can find my own way out," Theo snapped.

Fine! If they didn't want him, if he was getting in the way, then he would leave. Right now. Theo marched out of the room and headed for the front door. He could sense Ricky and Bullet watching him. He fully intended to keep going without a backward glance. He fully intended to take a leaf out of Mrs Marriott's book and leave the front door wide open, but somehow it didn't happen.

"I'll see you both at school then?" Theo turned and asked uncertainly.

Relief broadened Bullet's smile. Standing slightly behind Bullet, Ricky shrugged apologetically. He obviously had no idea why Bullet wanted him to stay behind. With a nod, Theo left the apartment, shutting the door quietly behind him.

14. No Doubt

Theo watched the classroom door like a circling hawk watching a rabbit. Where were Ricky and Bullet? What if something had happened to them? First Angela, then Ricky and Bullet. Theo felt like he was losing sight of all of them. The previous night, Theo had phoned Angela's foster mum and dad to find out how Angela was doing but there'd been no answer. In the end, Theo had phoned the hospital but all they would say was that Angela was comfortable.

"Theo? Why has the door suddenly become so fascinating?"

"Sorry, Mrs Daltry?" Theo snapped back to the here and now.

"You've been staring at that door for the last ten minutes. What am I missing?" asked the teacher.

"Nothing, Mrs Daltry. I… I was just thinking," Theo said quickly.

"Could you think by staring at the whiteboard instead of the door, please?"

"Sorry!" Theo mumbled. He turned to the whiteboard, making a great show of reading every letter Mrs Daltry had written. She raised her eyebrows but didn't say anything.

Where *were* they? If anything had happened to them… At that moment, the door opened slowly. Ricky and Bullet immediately entered the room and made a beeline for their chairs as if hoping the teacher wouldn't notice them.

"Excuse me! What time in the morning do you two call this?" asked Mrs Daltry.

"Sorry, Mrs Daltry," Ricky began.

"We … we missed our bus," Bullet added.

"Ricky, since when do you need a bus to get to school? You live two streets away."

Ricky and Bullet exchanged a quick look. "I went to meet Bullet," Ricky tried to explain. "So I had to get a bus to his house and then a bus back here again."

"The next time, let Toby come to school on his own. Then you'll both be on time," Mrs Daltry said, annoyed. "Now hurry up and sit down."

Ricky quickly sat down next to Theo. Bullet sat at his table.

"Everything OK?" Theo whispered.

"So-so," Ricky whispered back. "Ssh! I'll tell you later."

"I'd appreciate that," Mrs Daltry drawled from the front of the classroom.

Theo bent his head over his work. The last thing any of them wanted or needed right now was to antagonize Mrs Daltry and her bat ears!

Theo turned in his seat the moment Mrs Daltry was out the door, her bag of liquorice allsorts in her hands already. Most of the others in the class were close behind. "OK, give! What's going on?"

"Bullet wanted to talk to me about something. But that's not the important thing right now," Ricky dismissed with a wave of his hand. "Theo, the thing is, you were right. We *are* being followed. Someone followed us to school."

Icy drips careened down Theo's back. "Are you sure?"

"No doubt about it," Bullet replied, joining them.

"So what do we do?" Theo asked.

"I don't know," Bullet admitted.

The three friends looked at each other. No one wanted to say out loud what each of them had in their minds.

"What was this morning all about?" asked Theo at last.

"Pardon?"

"Why did you want Ricky to stay behind at your dad's flat?" asked Theo.

"This was one of the reasons." Bullet pulled a scrunched up, grubby envelope out of his duffle bag and passed it to Theo. Gingerly, Theo fished the letter from its envelope. Holding it by its corners, Theo regarded Bullet, who looked away. Theo unfolded the sheet of paper and began to read the two typed lines in the middle of the page.

Toby Barker,
Be careful you don't get stung.

Theo turned to Bullet. "What is this supposed to mean?"

Bullet shrugged. "I think it's meant to be a threat." At Theo's puzzled frown, Bullet continued. "The person who sent it obviously knows that I'm allergic to wasp stings."

Theo stared at the piece of paper before him, before turning back to Bullet. "D'you really think that's what it means?" he asked, aghast.

Bullet shrugged. "I can't think what else it could be referring to."

"Who knows you're allergic to wasp stings?"

"Mum and you guys. Family and friends. It's not a secret. I have to walk around with a hypo of adrenaline and wear a medic alert bracelet – you know that."

"So anyone could've found out," Theo mused. "What're you going to do about this letter?"

"See if I get any more."

"When did you get this one?" Theo asked, reading it one more time before handing it back.

"Yesterday," Bullet replied.

"But yesterday was a Sunday. The postman doesn't deliver on a Sunday," said Theo.

"It was hand delivered some time yesterday morning, apparently. It was waiting for me when I went home to get my school bag, " Bullet explained.

"Let me see the envelope again," said Theo.

Bullet handed it over. Theo scrutinized the back and the front of the envelope. It was a plain white, self-seal envelope with the words "Toby Barker" typed on the front and underlined. There was no address and no stamp.

"Why couldn't you have mentioned this at your dad's flat? Why did I have to leave?"

Theo didn't miss the conspiratorial glance which flashed between Ricky and Bullet. "What're you two not telling me?" Theo hoped his voice didn't sound as hurt at the exclusion as he felt.

Silence.

"You're not going to tell me, are you?"

"It was nothing to do with you, Theo," said Bullet. "Not really. I just wanted Ricky's advice on something."

Theo had to bite back his retort that his advice was every bit as good as Ricky's. If Bullet wanted to confide in Ricky about something and not him, then he'd just have to leave them to it.

"I suppose I'd be wasting my breath asking you to go to the police?"

Theo had his answer from the expression on Bullet's face.

"Aren't you frightened?" Theo asked, more than a hint of exasperation in his voice. "First Angela's accident and now this. If it was me I'd be camped on the doorstep of my local police station. You wouldn't be able to get me out of there."

"It's not that simple."

"It is from where I'm standing," Theo dismissed.

"But you don't have your dad to consider from where you're standing," said Bullet.

"Pass that by me again." Theo frowned in an effort to unravel Bullet's sentence.

"I mean, if someone's after my dad, then I want to be there to help, not locked up under police protection somewhere. Dad doesn't know about this and I want to keep it that way," said Bullet. "And besides, if I'm out and about, then maybe whoever it is will concentrate on me and leave my dad alone."

Stunned, Theo turned to see what was Ricky's reaction to all this. Ricky was slowly shaking his head.

"You're not thinking or saying anything that I haven't," Ricky sighed. "Bullet's determined not to get the police involved – at least not yet."

"Bullet, I'm sure your dad can look after himself much better than you can." Theo couldn't let it rest there. He had to try and make Bullet see sense.

"He needs me."

Not as much as you need him. The words almost fell out of Theo's mouth but he managed to bite them back just in time.

"Bullet, I'm sorry but I think this has gone far enough. If you won't go to the police then I will." Theo made up his mind.

"No!" Bullet exploded. "I don't want you to."

"It's for your own good. I'd never forgive myself if something happened to you or any of us."

"It won't."

"Oh, you can guarantee that, can you?" Theo said with sarcasm.

"It won't," Bullet repeated.

"And I'm going to make sure of that. As soon as school is over this afternoon I'm going straight to the police..."

"And what're you going to tell them?" Bullet drew himself up. His eyes took on a steely glint.

"I'll tell them about that letter for a start." Theo was well aware that he was about to lose a friend – and maybe for good – but what choice did he have? If Bullet wouldn't go to the police, then he would.

"What letter?" asked Bullet.

"The letter in your hand." Theo pointed.

"What letter?" Bullet asked again.

"That one..." Theo's voice trailed off as he realized what Bullet was up to.

"I don't know what you're talking about. I never received any letter," Bullet stated as if to drive the point home.

Theo and Bullet glared at each other without even blinking. Suddenly Theo made a lunge for the letter in Bullet's hand. Bullet pulled his hand away, jumping backwards at the same time. Theo only just missed – but miss he did.

"You try that again and I'll..."

"You'll what?" Theo challenged. "You're acting like a real..."

"Look, this isn't getting us anywhere," Ricky intervened. "If Bullet doesn't want to go to the police then we need to come up with a different strategy."

"You can't agree with what he's doing?" Theo asked, aghast.

"That's not the point, is it?" Ricky shook his head. "The police are out. So what do we do to flush out the person who's behind all this? That's what we have to work together to decide."

Casting a filthy look in Bullet's direction, Theo swallowed the anger rising in him like bile and sought to control his temper. "Will someone *please* tell me what's going on?"

"We've told you all you need to know, Theo," Ricky said quietly. "Let it go."

"Oi! You three. You know you're not allowed to be in here during breaktime." Mr Appleyard the caretaker stood at the open classroom door, waving them out.

Theo looked around. They were alone. Everyone else had left the classroom. Theo had been so wrapped up in what was going on with Bullet and Ricky that he hadn't even noticed.

"Come on. I haven't got all day," Mr Appleyard snapped.

Theo followed Ricky and Bullet out of the classroom, but the caretaker was way down the list of things on his mind. Ricky and

Bullet had all his attention. Why was he being excluded? What were they up to?

"I know how we can go forward from here," Bullet said as they left the classroom and Mr Appleyard behind. "I think we should go and see my dad after school."

"Your dad? You mean at his office?" Theo questioned.

Bullet nodded. "It's not far. And that way we'll have the chance to see the people he works with. I'll phone him this lunch-time and arrange it. Agreed?"

"Agreed." Ricky spoke for both himself and Theo.

And Theo couldn't help resenting it. And the way they told him some bits and kept other bits secret. But going to Mr Marriott's was a good idea and as he couldn't come up with a better one, he kept quiet.

The next step was to suss out Mr Marriott's colleagues and once that was done, then they'd all be in a better position to figure out who wanted Darius Marriott and Bullet permanently out of the way.

15. Office Life

"Can we see Mr Marriott, please?" Bullet asked.

"Mr Marriott? Mr Darius Marriott?" the receptionist questioned.

Theo glared at her. How many Mr Marriotts did they have in the building, for goodness' sake?

"Yes, that's right. Can we see him, please? He's expecting us," said Bullet.

"He is?"

"That's right. He's my dad." Pride laced every beaming word. Theo smiled faintly to himself but said nothing. Maybe, in spite of everything, this would work out OK for Bullet after all.

"Just a moment." The receptionist picked up the phone receiver and pressed four numbers in quick succession. She gave the three boys a suspicious look before swivelling her chair away from them and cupping her hand over the mouth piece before she spoke.

Theo raised his eyes heavenward. This woman wouldn't have been out of place working for the American CIA.

"What's your name?" the receptionist asked Bullet.

"Toby. Toby Barker."

"And your names?"

"I'm Ricky Burridge and this is Theo Mosley," said Ricky.

The receptionist swivelled her chair away from them again. She whispered into the telephone receiver, nodding, then shaking her head as she spoke. A few moments later she put down the receiver, a look of surprise on her face. "Take the lift up to the third floor. You'll be met."

"Thank you." Bullet smiled, more than a hint of smugness turning up his lips.

Theo and Ricky followed Bullet to the lift.

Theo turned to look out of the glass-fronted reception area into the street beyond.

"What's the matter?" Ricky asked.

"D'you think we're still being followed?" Theo asked tentatively.

Ricky turned to look out into the street too. "I don't know. If we are being followed then they've got better at it."

Theo nodded his agreement as they all stepped into the lift. Ricky checked the buttons in the lift. "Seven floors! Does the whole building belong to your dad?"

Bullet nodded.

"Wow!" Ricky whistled, impressed.

They entered the lift and headed up to the third floor.

"Why are we here again?" Theo asked dryly.

"Moral support," Bullet answered at once. "Plus three heads are better than two or one."

"You didn't think that earlier this morning," Theo muttered.

"Pardon?"

"Nothing." Theo looked away from the speculative glance being directed at him by

Ricky. Theo knew he was being silly, but he couldn't help it. Being excluded still rankled. The lift doors opened and they all stepped out.

"Hi. Toby?" A woman with impossibly red hair and a wide smile beamed at all of them.

"Yes, I'm Toby." Bullet put out his hand.

"And Ricky?"

Ricky nodded.

"And you must be Theo."

"That's right." Theo nodded as well.

"Welcome. Darius said you might be popping in this afternoon for a tour. I'm Joanne Fleming. Call me Jo – everyone does. It's great to meet all of you at last. Toby, Darius has told me so much about you."

"Has he?" Bullet was pleased.

"Are you kidding? He's spoken of nothing else. I must admit, it was a bit of a surprise for all of us when we heard he had a son. A long-lost son you might say. But now he's found you – or you found him." Jo grinned.

Ricky and Theo exchanged a glance. Goodness, but this woman could chat! She hardly paused to draw breath. But Theo liked her! She was friendly and bubbly. Theo suspected that most people would like this woman. They walked through the double doors at the end of the short corridor to find themselves in a large, open plan area with offices running down one side of it.

"Let me introduce you to some of the people your dad works with." Jo walked almost as quickly as she talked. Theo had to practically trot to keep up with her. "This is Yves Hamilton's office. He's our Sales and Marketing Director."

They approached an office with a wooden door and fluted, frosted windows on either side of it. Jo rapped smartly on the door and, without waiting for a reply, opened it immediately.

A black man with short hair at the sides and no hair at all on top, turned around in his chair to face them, his fingers still poised over his computer keyboard. He wore gold-rimmed glasses which dominated his face. His jacket was slung over his chair and his sleeves were rolled up to his elbows.

"Hi, Yves. This is Toby, Darius's son, and his friends, Ricky and Theo."

"Is it now? Hi, there." Yves stretched out his hand to Bullet, who shook it. He waved to Theo and Ricky who stood behind Bullet, out of reach. "So what brings the three of you to this neck of the woods?"

"Dad said he'd show us around."

"Ah yes! Your dad warned ... told us about changing his will. So I suppose it's only right. All this is going to be yours one day." Yves smiled.

Bullet returned the smile uneasily. "Not for years and years yet."

Yves nodded but didn't reply.

"So what exactly do you do, Mr Hamilton?" Theo asked.

Yves looked at Theo with surprise. Theo realized that the man had forgotten he was standing there. Bullet had all of his attention.

"I'm in charge of making sure that we market and sell our products in the most cost-effective, efficient and profitable way possible." Yves smiled.

"D'you do that all by yourself?"

Yves burst out laughing. "Thank you for your confidence in my super-human abilities but no, I don't. I have a team of about one hundred and thirty in this country alone. The sales staff are based at our other offices up and down the country, although most of the marketing staff are based in this building."

"Didn't I see you a couple of weeks ago at our school when Mr Marriott came for a visit?" bluffed Theo.

Yves Hamilton's smile vanished. "That was the morning Darius had his heart attack, wasn't it?"

Theo nodded.

"You couldn't have seen me. I was in a marketing strategy meeting all morning."

"My mistake." Theo shrugged. "I thought I saw you there but I've obviously got it wrong."

"Jo, you were there, weren't you?" Yves turned to Darius's personal assistant.

"Yep! At the back of the hall watching. Faith was there too – which is just as well because when it all happened, I'm afraid I lost it. Faith accompanied Darius to the hospital and I came back here. It gave me quite a shock to see Darius keel over like that, I can tell you." Jo shrugged. "Thank goodness he's OK now."

"I still think he should be taking it easy. He's trying to do too much." Yves shook his head.

"You know Darius," Jo smiled. "The doctor at the hospital told him that it probably wasn't a heart attack so he signs himself out and he's back to work the following week. You can't keep a good man down!"

"Well, I'll tell you what I told him. He's being too hasty. He should give himself time to recover. If it wasn't his heart giving him a warning, then it was something going wrong somewhere in his body. You don't just hit the deck for no reason. He needs to slow down."

"Yes, Yves. I'm sure Toby and his friends didn't come here to hear your views on Darius's health."

Yves Hamilton looked at Toby sheepishly. "I guess I'm just a fusser at heart! It's just that your dad is not only my work colleague but a very good friend. I'd hate to see anything happen to him."

"Well, sorry to interrupt you, Yves. I'll let you get on with it. Next stop – Faith Shanley's office. She's our R&D director."

At Ricky's puzzled look, Theo supplied, "Research and Development director."

"Oh." Ricky nodded his thanks.

They moved along to the next office. There was no need to knock, for this door was already open.

"Hi, Faith."

Faith Shanley slammed shut the drawer she'd been rummaging in before she looked up. She was pretty in a cold, detached sort of way. She had jet black hair and the lightest blue eyes Theo had ever seen. They were so light as to be almost colourless. It gave her the strangest appearance.

"Are you busy?" Jo smiled.

"Yes I am, actually," Faith declared icily. She glared at Toby, then Ricky and Theo.

"This is Toby Barker, Darius's son. And these are his friends, Theo and Ricky."

Faith Shanley continued to scrutinize them all without saying a word. Finally she barked out, "Shouldn't you three be in school?"

"School's over for today," Bullet informed her.

"Already? It's only four-thirty."

"School finishes at three-thirty."

"That early? No wonder you children leave school not knowing your backside from a hole in the ground!" Faith snorted with disgust.

Charming! Theo glared at the R&D director. With her people skills – or the lack of them – Theo wouldn't let her direct traffic, much less the research and development department.

"Jo mentioned that you were at our school when Darius collapsed on our school stage." Ricky shook his head. "It must have given you quite a shock."

"I was in the car waiting for him. The first I knew about it was when the ambulance pulled up." Faith frowned. "I promised myself when I left school that I'd never set foot in another one and I'm a woman of my word."

"Yes, er ... I can see you're busy, so we'll leave you to it." Jo hustled them out of Faith's office and moved them down to the next one. "Don't mind Faith. She's been a bit ... preoccupied over the last couple of weeks."

Theo looked at all the secretaries and other workers busy at their computers in the open plan office. Talk about living in each other's pockets. In the open plan you couldn't even make a phone call with any degree of privacy. He'd hate to work anywhere quite that exposed. Anyway, the situation wouldn't arise. He was going to be a world-famous, first-class detective.

"Now this is Ron Westall's office. He's the company secretary. I don't know if you know this Toby, but Ron started DemTech with your dad." Jo popped her head around the door and looked around the empty office. "Now where's he got to?"

Jo straightened up to look around the rest of the open plan. "Oh well! He'll turn up."

"If Ron Westall started the company with Mr Marriott, why does DemTech stand for Darius Evan Marriott Technologies?" Theo asked.

"I'll answer that," a voice piped up from behind them.

Theo swung around. An older man than Darius with chestnut-brown, wavy hair, twinkling blue eyes and a friendly face grinned at them. The silvery strands in his hair were many. He kept running his fingers through his hair in an effort to stop it flopping down over his face.

"I'm Ron Westall. And to answer your question, I've always been a 'get on with it behind the scenes' kind of guy. Darius has always been better at presenting our ideas than me, so I let him get on with it. But the first couple of successful inventions DemTech engineered were based on ideas I had. I had the ideas, Darius put up all the money. Another reason the company is named after him."

"But we couldn't do without you." Jo smiled.

"Jo, you're too good to me." Ron's smile broadened.

"Are you going to the dance on Saturday?" Jo asked.

"Will you be there?"

Jo nodded.

"Then of course I will," Ron beamed.

"Ron, you are such a flirt," Jo said dryly.

"What dance?" Theo whispered to Bullet.

"It's the DemTech annual company summer dance. They're all going to some swish hotel," Bullet whispered back.

"Jo, d'you know if Yves and Faith are going on Saturday night?" asked Ron.

"They both said they were – although Faith said she might have to duck out early."

"She always says that, and then she's one of the last ones to leave!" Ron chuckled. "Anyway, I'd better get back to my office. I wouldn't want to be accused of slacking."

Ron walked off with a wave. Jo carried on walking down the corridor formed by the offices on one side and half-partitions on the other. "This office at the end here belongs to your dad. I think his wife is in there at the moment but I'm sure she won't be too long."

They all stopped outside Darius's closed door. Theo could hear Samantha Marriott's muffled voice through the door and she didn't sound happy.

"I don't think so..." Samantha's voice was becoming louder and more shrill.

Theo heard the lower baritone of Darius's voice, although he couldn't make out the words.

"You can't do this to me, Darius." Samantha's words rang out loud and clear. "I won't be treated like a pair of old shoes."

"At least old shoes were once of some use. You're just..." The rest of Darius's inaudible answer seemed to make things worse, not better.

"I'll make you pay for this – I swear I will." Samantha was practically screaming by now.

Without warning, the door burst open and Samantha came careering out to crash straight into Jo.

"Did you have a good time, listening at the key-hole?" Samantha sneered.

"I did no such thing, Mrs Marriott," Jo replied evenly. "We were just waiting for you to come out."

Only then did Samantha realize that Jo wasn't alone. Her eyes narrowed into wafer thin slivers of dislike when she saw Toby.

"Come to inspect your inheritance, have you? Let's hope you live long enough to enjoy it."

"Mrs Marriott, I think that's enough," Jo said quietly.

"Who d'you think you're talking to?" Samantha rounded on the PA. "You're just the hired help around here and don't you forget that."

"Jo is absolutely right." Darius's ice-cold voice piped up from behind his wife. "That will be quite enough."

The look Samantha Marriott directed at first her husband and then Jo was scalding. Without another word she marched off.

"Don't take any notice of Samantha." Darius smiled at Toby. "She's a toothless dog with a very loud voice! Come in. Come in! Welcome. Thanks, Jo." Darius shut the door after Ricky had entered the room, leaving Jo outside.

"Have you just arrived? What've you seen so far?"

"Jo introduced us to the other directors of DemTech," said Bullet.

Darius smiled. "Good! Now then ... let's see... How would you like to see our research and development labs? I'll show you where we're testing the Lazarus suit."

"That'd be great, Dad," Bullet enthused.

"Yeah. Thank you, Mr Marriott," said Ricky.

Theo nodded his thanks. This Darius Marriott was a world apart from the one in the hospital. Maybe the last couple of weeks spent with Bullet had started to mellow him out a bit.

"This way then," said Darius, cheerfully.

They all trooped after him as he led the way to the lifts.

"Er, Darius, you have the Chivers meeting in less than five minutes." Jo came running after him.

"Make them comfortable and tell them I'll

be with them in about fifteen minutes," Darius said.

"But Mr Chivers..."

"Jo..." Darius's smile had disappeared.

Jo's sunny expression shut up like a pen-knife. "Yes of course, Darius." She nodded quickly. And she scurried back to her table outside Darius's office.

"Sorry about that." The smile appeared again.

As they stepped into the lift, Theo cast Darius a speculative look. This man was a right Janus – a man with two faces. The public face he used to impress people and make the world think he was wonderful, but his private face was a lot nastier. And Theo knew which one he believed to be Darius Marriott's true face.

He risked a look at Bullet who was laughing at some joke his dad had just told him. Even Ricky was laughing. They might have been fooled by Darius's act but Theo most certainly wasn't. Darius might have acknowledged Bullet openly as his son, he might even have left him an awful lot of money in his will, but there was more to it than that. All this was moving much, much too fast. The introductions, the will-changing, the invites to DemTech and the apartment. It was as if Darius wanted the whole world to know that he was accepting his son with open arms. But Theo just couldn't shake the feeling that Darius was up to something. Something which might cost all of them, but especially Bullet, very dear indeed.

16. Opinions

"Here we are! Seventh floor! Everyone out." Darius was the last one out of the lift. "This way to the labs."

The more Darius spoke, the less impressed Theo was with him. "I don't know who he thinks he's fooling with his *Willy Wonka* impersonation," Theo thought with a scowl.

"This floor contains our testing labs. The sixth and seventh floors of this building are used for research and development in its initial stages. I have other R&D facilities up and down the country, of course."

"Of course," Theo muttered.

Darius and Bullet turned to look at him. Darius's smile wavered only slightly.

"Anyway, at the moment the testing labs are all concentrating on the Lazarus suit," Darius continued.

"Which was your idea, Mr Marriott — wasn't it?" Theo asked politely.

"Yes, as a matter of fact it was," Darius replied, his mask of bonhomie never slipping.

"Aren't you afraid someone will try to steal your idea?" Ricky asked.

"Not with the security I have in this building. People know about the Lazarus suit now, of course. It was officially announced over a month ago now. But they don't know about any of the components or the technology used. I'm sure any number of my competitors would sell their souls for one of our prototype suits but it's not going to happen."

Ricky looked around, scepticism on his face.

"All the doors are solid wood and steel with locking mechanisms we designed ourselves here at DemTech. The windows are all made of toughened glass so that nothing short of rapid machine gun fire at close range could make so much as a dent in them. Believe me, no one's walking out of this building with anything that doesn't belong to them – and the Lazarus suit is *mine*."

Darius opened the nearest door to the lift. Three people occupied the room – one man and two women, each wearing white overalls. One sat at a computer, the other two sat at the huge table in the middle of the room. Three or four computers were situated on the only other table against the far wall. Books lined one set of shelves and electronic instruments lined another. High up on the wall there was a ventilation grille, about three times the size of the one in the bathroom in Theo's house. A fire extinguisher and a smoke alarm where the glass had to be broken to raise the alarm were hidden away in one corner of the room. The occupants of the room sat on padded wooden stools which didn't look at all comfortable.

That's probably Darius Marriott making the chairs uncomfy to make sure that no one falls asleep on the job, Theo thought.

"Hi, Sam. How's it going?" Darius asked the man at the middle table.

"Fine thanks, Mr Marriott," Sam replied. "The testing is going very smoothly indeed."

"That's what I like to hear." Darius rubbed his hands together. "So we're still on schedule?"

"Yes, sir. No problem."

"How do you test something like the Lazarus suit?" Theo couldn't help asking. "I mean, don't you need people to act as guinea pigs?"

The room went strangely quiet at that. Tense moments passed, before Darius laughed lightly.

"We test it as much as we can using computer simulations. And we have anatomically correct robots or dummies which are programmed to display any number of symptoms for our Lazarus suits to deal with."

"Oh I see," Theo said doubtfully.

He wondered what he had said to make everyone pause like that.

"And these suits are just for presidents and prime ministers and that?"

"Not at all. Our suits come in all shapes and sizes," Darius denied.

"They're for anyone who can afford them," a woman piped up from across the room in front of a computer.

Darius turned and lasered her with his look. The woman immediately turned back to her computer, suddenly very busy.

"Dad, can we see some of your other labs?" Bullet asked quickly.

Darius started, almost as if he'd forgotten about them for a moment. "Yes, of course. Right this way."

Darius took them into some more of the labs on the seventh floor. In one lab, a short woman was putting on a Lazarus suit, adjusting the straps across her chest and waist to ensure a snug fit.

"How d'you know which medications to put in the suit?" Bullet asked.

"That's all worked out beforehand, based on each individual's medical history," Darius answered.

"And how d'you set it up?"

Theo frowned at Bullet. Why did he want to know that? What difference did it make? Bullet turned to face Theo as if he'd heard the unspoken questions.

"Just interested," he said, defensively.

Darius proceeded to explain exactly how the appropriate syringes with the necessary medication should be attached to the suit.

"And my suit will do the rest," he finished with a flourish.

"It's a very, very clever idea, Dad," Bullet enthused. "I hope I can come up with something half as good when I'm an inventor."

By the time Darius had showed them around the R&D labs on the sixth floor as well, Theo had to admit he was very impressed. The testing labs were like nothing he'd ever imagined. One contained a mock-up of an intensive care hospital ward, another contained a number of different-sized suits at various stages of development and all the labs contained more electronic gadgetry than Theo had ever seen in his life.

"This lot must've cost a fortune," Theo whistled. For the first time he was beginning to appreciate just how rich Darius Marriott really was.

"DemTech have spent over twenty million on the Lazarus suit already," Darius shrugged. "But it's all going to be worth it."

Theo nodded. He could well believe it. He wouldn't have minded being shown the whole lot again as it was a lot to take in at just one go, but unfortunately it was getting late.

"Thank you so much for showing us around, Mr Marriott," Ricky said sincerely. "It was great – really interesting."

"My pleasure," Darius smiled, escorting them back to the lift. "It's the least I could do. After all, you did help to save my life."

"Oh yes! By the way, Mr Marriott, did the police ever tell you what was in that hypodermic syringe left by the bogus doctor?" asked Theo.

Darius's expression immediately became strangely watchful. "Ever the detective, eh! As a matter of fact, they did tell me. Apparently it was potassium chloride. It would've made my heart stop almost immediately and everyone would've assumed I'd had another heart attack – fatal this time."

"So someone was still trying to make it look like an accident," Theo mused to himself.

"Well, at least all that nonsense is over now." Darius's smile missed his eyes by kilometres. "So thank you for your concern but there's no need to worry."

"Did the police catch the person responsible, then?" Ricky asked.

"No, I did," Darius replied.

Theo and Ricky stared at him, astounded.

"Bullet didn't tell us the person who tried to harm you had been arrested." Ricky faced Bullet with accusatory eyes.

"I didn't know," said Bullet. "But I'm so glad, Dad."

"You must be very relieved." Theo thought about how he'd feel if he had the sword of Damocles suddenly removed from over his head. Relief wouldn't begin to describe it.

"Yes. It is good news," Darius agreed evenly.

Good news! Is that all he had to say? Good news? Theo looked at Darius suspiciously and all at once he knew beyond a shadow of a doubt that Darius was lying. But why? *Why?*

"I was sorry to hear about your friend's accident. Toby tells me the driver jumped a red light and hit Angela and never stopped."

"I don't understand. What...?"

A swift elbow in the ribs from Ricky halted the rest of Theo's sentence.

"Yeah! I don't understand how anyone could do something like that either," Ricky said. "But at least Angela's doing OK in hospital. We're going to visit her tomorrow."

"Give her my best, won't you," said Darius.

Ricky nodded.

"So you're all off home now?" Darius asked as the lift arrived.

"Yes."

"That's right."

"What about you, Toby? Will you be having dinner at my apartment or with your mum? I'll give you a lift home afterwards if you have dinner with me."

Bullet thought for a while. "With Mum I think."

"Then I'll see you all soon," Darius said.

"Oh, hang on. Sorry, Dad. I've left my duffle bag in lab number four. I'll just go and get it." And before anyone could say a word, Bullet was off. An embarrassed silence descended as they all tried to find something to say.

"How did you catch the person who tried to ... harm you?" Theo asked at last.

"I don't think I should say. It's now in the hands of the police and I'm not supposed to talk about it until after the court case," Darius replied.

Or at least until you've had a chance to make up a reasonable story, Theo thought, making sure his expression stayed perfectly neutral.

"Have all those people in the offices on the same floor as you been at this company a long time?" asked Theo.

Darius didn't attempt to hide the

suspicious look on his face. "Ron and I started the company and Faith and Yves came on board within the first year."

"It's lucky it wasn't any of them, then." Theo decided to try his luck.

"None of them have any reason to try and get rid of me. They all have plenty of shares in the company and they're each paper millionaires because of it. Even Jo my secretary has shares in DemTech. She's a very rich woman too."

"What's a paper millionaire?" Theo asked.

Darius looked annoyed. "It means that they all have shares which are worth a great deal of money if they were to sell them – which they can't."

"Why not?"

"Because the shares were signed over to them on the strict understanding that each of the shareholders had to hold on to their shares for a minimum of fifteen years. They all signed contracts to that effect. I'm not having DemTech carved up by big conglomerates trying to buy all the shares they can, so that they can take over my company. And if any of the other stock holders so much as live together, never mind get married, one of the parties has to give up all rights to their shares. In effect the shares come back to me."

"So if Yves and Faith or Ron and Faith get married, one of them loses their shares? Is that right?" Theo wanted to make sure that he hadn't misunderstood.

Darius nodded. "Correct. The person with the largest amount of shares has to give them back to me."

"And if something should happen to you?" asked Ricky.

"Then of course my fifty-one percent stock holding in the company goes to Toby. But nothing is going to happen to me. I intend to be around for a very, very long time."

"Of course," Theo said. But before he could say anything else, Bullet appeared.

"Here it is. I've found it." He held up his bulging duffle bag.

They all trooped into the lift.

"Toby, phone me tomorrow and let me know how you are – OK?"

Bullet nodded. "See you, Dad."

And the lift doors shut.

"I'm glad everything's worked out OK between you and your dad," Theo said carefully.

Bullet and Ricky exchanged a glance. Neither of them spoke. Once again, Theo found himself wondering just what on earth was going on.

17. Visiting Hours

"Hi, Angela. We can't stay long. How're you feeling?"

"Why can't you stay long? You've only just got here." Angela struggled to sit up a bit more. "And you lot took your time visiting me. I was beginning to wonder if I had bad breath or something!"

"You've finally guessed, huh!" Ricky grinned.

Angela's look spoke unspoken volumes!

"I see you're back to normal," Theo said dryly.

"All apart from my leg here." Angela pointed to the plaster cast which covered most of her right leg.

"How does it feel?" Ricky asked.

"Itchy! What's the matter with you, Bullet? You're very quiet."

Bullet looked at the curtains surrounding Angela's bed, he looked up and down the hospital ward, he looked everywhere but directly at Angela.

"I ... er ... I just wanted..."

"You wanted to get down on bended knee and kiss my itchy big toe and thank me for saving your life." Angela grinned.

Urrgghhh! Theo broke out in a cold sweat at the thought of it.

"Well, I wouldn't go that far," Bullet laughed, now looking at Angela.

"But something like that – right?"

"Something like that," Bullet agreed.

"So how have you lot been getting on without me? Have you made any progress?"

"Some," Ricky said after a brief glance at Bullet.

"But not as much as we should have made by now," Theo added.

"Let's hear it then," Angela prompted.

They spent the next ten minutes arguing

about what had happened after Angela was taken to hospital, bringing Angela up-to-date with everything that had taken place.

"So who's on our list of suspects?" asked Angela.

Bullet and Ricky turned expectantly to Theo. "I think it has to be someone who'd benefit from Darius Marriott's death."

"You had to read fifty million 'How To Be A Detective' books to reach that conclusion?" Angela was not impressed.

"If you'll let me finish!" Theo sniffed. "As I see it, that narrows our list of suspects down to Darius Marriott's wife, Samantha; Ron Westall, the company secretary; Faith Shanley, the R&D director; or Yves Hamilton, the sales and marketing director. Now, they each get another block of shares when Darius dies but not enough for any one of them to get controlling interest of DemTech. That would stay with Bullet here. He'll get fifty-one percent of all the shares in the company which means it'll be his. But if something happens to Bullet and his dad, then the co-directors of DemTech are laughing."

"What about Jo Fleming?" Ricky frowned.

"What about her?" asked Theo.

"Well, she's got some shares in the company too – remember?" Ricky pointed out.

"Oh yes ... I'd forgotten about her."

"So who do you think is responsible for all this?" asked Angela.

"I don't know," Theo replied slowly. "I still can't get over the feeling that I'm missing something – something obvious and vital. I know it has to be one of the directors of the company or Samantha Marriott but I still can't work out who. At the moment Faith Shanley's my favourite suspect."

"Why?" Bullet asked, surprised.

"She looks and acts like she could wrestle a shark with one hand tied behind her back," Theo said.

"That doesn't make her a killer," Ricky pointed out.

"So who do you think it is, then?" asked Theo.

"Someone else," Ricky said mysteriously.

"Like who?"

Ricky shook his head, unwilling to say anything further.

"Come on, Ricky. Stop being so mysterious," Angela cajoled.

"It's just that I've been doing a little detective work of my own," Ricky admitted. "And I suspect something about one of DemTech's directors."

"What?" Theo asked, exasperated.

"I'm not going to say until I have proof." Ricky shook his head.

"Ricky, this is Theo, Bullet and Angela you're talking to," Theo said, annoyed. "You don't need concrete proof to make us believe you."

"I know. But if what I suspect is true, then I want to be sure of my facts." When Theo opened his mouth to argue further, Ricky stated, "Theo, Darius Marriott is Bullet's dad. I want to be absolutely certain I'm not making a mistake before I do anything to upset either of them or jeopardize their relationship."

"And might it come to that?" Bullet asked quietly.

Ricky didn't answer. The look on his face said that he thought he'd said too much already.

"What I will say is this," Ricky said at last. "Bullet, you're not to trust any of the staff at DemTech. If anyone, anyone at all, from that company phones you and says they want to see you — for whatever reason — make sure you take one of us along with you. D'you understand?"

Bullet nodded.

"This is really important, Bullet. D'you understand me? You're not to trust anyone from DemTech."

"I get it. I get it." Bullet frowned.

Everyone stared at Ricky. None of them had ever before heard that note of urgency in his voice.

"Ricky, stop it." Bullet frowned. "You're ... you're making me nervous."

"I hope so," Ricky said seriously. "I really hope so. 'Cause if you don't do as I say — it'll probably be the last thing you ever do."

Theo wasn't going to let him get away with that. "Ricky, d'you remember when Jade was convinced her dead dad was sending her e-mail messages and I thought I'd discovered who the real culprit was?" Theo reminded his friend. "I set a trap to catch him and I didn't tell you what I was doing."

Ricky's lips thinned. He knew what was coming next.

"D'you remember how you went ballistic when you found out what I'd done?" Theo continued relentlessly. "And now you're doing exactly the same thing. If it wasn't OK for me, how come you can do it?"

"I was wondering that myself," Angela piped up.

"I agree with Theo." Bullet put in his five pence worth. "And this has more to do with me than any of you. I don't think you should shut me out like this."

Theo glared at Bullet. There was a lot of shutting out going on. Ricky looked at Angela lying on her hospital bed and then at Theo and Bullet. "It's just that... OK. I was planning on going to the Family Record Centre on Saturday."

"The what?"

"The Family Record Centre in Islington. They keep records of all births, marriages and deaths in England and Wales. It used to be at St Catherine's House but now it's moved," Ricky explained.

"Why're you going there?" Theo questioned.

"To test a theory. And if my theory is right, then I'm hoping to set a trap for the ones doing this. I think that's the only way to flush them out."

"Are they open on Saturdays?" Theo asked.

Ricky nodded. "I checked."

"I'm going with you," Bullet said at once.

Looking straight at Ricky, Theo said, "So am I. And don't bother arguing because you'll just be wasting your breath."

"We can't all go. Bullet, you'd better stay behind," Ricky said.

"But..."

"We'll let you know what we found out as soon as we get back. I promise," Ricky interrupted. "You're going to have to trust us."

"What about this trap you're going to set? I can help with that, surely?" said Bullet.

"Actually, I did want you to do something for me..." Ricky admitted reluctantly. "Are you going to see your dad tomorrow?"

"Yeah. I was planning to pop into his office after school. Why?"

"I need you to spread some information about. The thing is, it'll be dangerous." Ricky's voice faded to a whisper.

"Just tell me what you want me to do," Bullet said with determination.

"We're going to set a trap," Ricky added sombrely. "But I'm worried we'll be the ones caught in it."

"Is that why you didn't want to include any of us?" Bullet asked. "Just in case things went wrong?"

"Yes. These people have already proved that they'll stop at nothing to get what they want. I just don't want any of us to get steam-rollered whilst we're trying to catch them out."

"But Dad said the police have already arrested the person behind all this," Bullet reminded them.

"If someone has been arrested for your dad's attempted murder, then the police have the wrong person. I'm sure of it." Ricky's voice was grim.

They all digested Ricky's last statement in silence.

"And you think more than one person is involved in this?" Bullet said.

Ricky nodded. "And I think they're covering each other's tracks, or your dad would've found them out by now."

"Is it two people who work for Dad?"

Ricky nodded. "I think so. And if I'm right, a visit to the Family Record Centre will prove it."

"And if you're wrong?" Angela asked.

"Then Bullet and his dad are in even more danger."

"How d'you work that out?" asked Theo.

"Because we'll have narrowed down our list of suspects and the person or people doing this will have to act even more quickly. Time will no longer be on our side," Ricky said. "You see, that's the problem. With all this, I might actually make things worse."

18. Bait

"I still can't believe it." Theo shook his head.

It was five-thirty in the evening. Ricky and Theo were on their way home from the Family / Record Centre, both their expressions grim. The tube train was jam-packed with late afternoon shoppers returning home and Ricky and Theo stood next to each other, squashed against the door.

"What made you suspect?" Theo couldn't keep the admiration out of his voice.

"Something she said – and watching the two of them together," Ricky replied.

"Well, they completely fooled me. Lucky you were more on the ball than I was,"

Theo said. Though he couldn't help feeling that in some way, he had failed. He should've been the one to make the connection. He should've picked up on the clues, too.

"Theo, it's not that I cracked it, or you cracked it. We solved this together." Ricky correctly interpreted the expression on his friend's face.

"It's not that so much. It's just that..."

"It's just that we make a good team," Ricky insisted.

Theo smiled. "That's exactly what I was going to say!"

"What we have to do now is use this information to drag them out into the open. We have to make them show their hand," said Ricky.

"How d'you intend to do that?"

"Bullet's already taken care of that bit back home," Ricky said with satisfaction.

Theo was startled. "He doesn't know..."

"No. How can he when we only found out for certain about an hour ago? But yesterday when he went to his dad's office, I asked him to tell everyone what you'd be up to this afternoon. He was to try and make sure that all the staff on the third floor of DemTech got to hear about your forthcoming visit to the Family Record Centre. I told him to make sure the info was given out in a casual way as if he was just making conversation."

"Hang on a minute. *My* visit?" Theo asked, astounded.

"Yes, you! That way we can use you as bait and I'll be there to make sure that nothing bad happens to you."

"Thank you very much!" Theo exploded. "If you're going to use me as bait, you could've told me first."

"I'm telling you now."

"Thanks for nothing. So when we get home, there could be some lunatic just waiting to run me down or blow me up or anything."

"It won't come to that – I told you. I'm here to make sure that you're perfectly safe."

"You can't guarantee that. Ricky, you..."

"This is where we get off. Come on."

Ricky pulled Theo past the already closing tube train doors. "I'll go with you to your house and then I'll disappear for half an hour if you don't mind."

"Why?"

"I've got one last thing to check at the library." Ricky glanced down at his watch. "And I'd better hurry up before it closes."

"What d'you need to check?"

"Some DemTech annual accounts information and I want to look up something on Darius Marriott."

"What?"

"I'll tell you once I've got the info."

"Oh Ricky, don't start all that again. I thought we'd got all this 'my surname is Secret and my middle name is Mystery' nonsense sorted out."

"I'll tell you when I've been to the library – not before," Ricky insisted stubbornly.

"Before you disappear, why exactly did Bullet want to talk to you alone in his dad's apartment the other day?" Theo couldn't help asking.

"He wanted my advice about something."

"I know that. What? And why didn't he want my advice too?"

Ricky sighed. "'Cause you live with your happily-married mum and dad. Bullet was like me until a couple of weeks ago. There was no dad on the scene."

"Oh..." Theo couldn't argue with that. "So what did Bullet ask you?"

"His dad wants Bullet to come and live with him permanently. Bullet just wanted to know what I'd do in his shoes. But I was sworn to secrecy, so don't go blabbing."

"Of course not." Theo frowned. "So what's Bullet going to do?"

"He's not sure. But he thinks he'll stay with his mum."

"Is that what you'd do?"

"Oh yes!" Ricky replied without a moment's hesitation.

There was something in his voice. Some strange hard edge that Theo hadn't heard before. "What's the matter?" Theo questioned.

Ricky shook his head.

"Come on. Something's obviously troubling you."

"Never mind. Just leave it," Ricky dismissed.

Theo glared at Ricky, oblivious to the impatient glances being directed at him by those trying to leave the station. Fine! If Ricky wanted to play that game then Theo wasn't about to spoil his fun.

"All right then. Be like that," Theo said at last.

They walked back to Theo's house, chatting about nothing in particular, rather than the subject uppermost in both their minds. Until, running out of things to say, they both fell silent. Theo couldn't understand what was going on with this whole business. For the last few days, he'd felt as if he was constantly fifteen minutes behind everyone else. Secrets... That was it. Everyone seemed to have secrets. And he was so close to what was going on, he felt as if he couldn't see the wood for the trees. He'd never really known what that saying meant before, but now its meaning was all too clear.

He was too close to Bullet and Ricky to see things objectively. Maybe that's why Ricky had had an inkling as to who might be responsible for all this mayhem before he had. He felt as if he'd done nothing but worry for longer than he cared to remember. He was worried about Bullet and Angela and Ricky and even Darius Marriott. Still, now that they had found the information they were looking for, maybe they could get somewhere at last. The proof of what they had found wouldn't be posted to them for another four or five days though. Finding the data on the Family Records computer was one thing. Getting a proper printout of that data was apparently something else entirely. They'd handed over their money, but they couldn't get the certificate they'd paid for, for a minimum of four days. Theo just hoped and prayed that they *had* four days. If Bullet had spread rumours about what he'd been doing that day, then even four hours seemed optimistic.

And at that moment, Theo made a decision. He'd go home and wait for Ricky. And then tomorrow without fail, they'd go to the police with what they knew. And if Bullet and Ricky wouldn't go with him, then he'd go by himself. He was no one's sitting duck and at the moment, that's exactly what he felt like. It wasn't a pleasant feeling. Theo quickly turned his head. There were people milling about here, there and everywhere. Was one of them watching him? What if he was being followed? What if...?

Stop it! Theo told himself firmly. He was OK. Even if Bullet had managed to pass on the message about his so-called solo trip to the Family Record Centre, there wouldn't have been time for the guilty parties to have arranged anything. He was safe – but only if he went to the police the very next morning. Now that the decision had been made, Theo felt strangely comforted. All he had to do was hold on for one more night.

Outside Theo's house, Ricky said, "Right then, now you're safely home, I'll see you in a little while. I've only got fifteen minutes before the library closes." And Ricky was already turning around and heading back the way they had just come.

"Ricky..." Theo called after him.

"Tell me later," Ricky called back, breaking into a run.

With a sigh, Theo turned and went into his house. He had a foot on the bottom step when his dad came out of the living-room.

"Hi, Theo. How was your day?"

"Informative," Theo told his dad. He headed up the stairs, pulling off his jacket as he went.

"Just a sec. You got a message from Bullet. He wants you to meet him at the DemTech building. He said he and his dad will meet you there and his dad will give you a lift home again," said Theo's dad. "I don't know what all of you have been up to recently but I do know that I've hardly seen you."

"When did Bullet phone?"

"About an hour ago. He said it was urgent."

Theo glanced at his watch. "I'm just going to pop out for a while. Dad, Ricky's going to come round later. When he does, could you tell him where I've gone and that I'll be back soon."

"All I seem to do around this house is take messages for you," Theo's dad grumbled. "And I never get one word of thanks either."

"Thank you for taking my messages, Dad," Theo said deliberately.

"It's too late." Theo's dad sniffed with mock indignation. "Thanks should be spontaneous, not prompted."

"Later, Dad," Theo called, as he headed out of the door.

"Not too much later, Theo," his dad called back at once. "I want you home within the hour – without fail. We'd see more of you if you were a lodger instead of our son. I don't know why your mum and me..."

Theo didn't hear any more. He walked briskly down the garden path, breaking into a run once he hit the road. He didn't know why Bullet wanted to see him but it was obviously important.

"Name?"

Theo stared at the intercom. He peered through the glass to look at the uniformed security guard who had asked the question.

"Name?" The voice came again, edged with impatience.

"Theo. Theo Mosley."

"Ah yes. You're expected," said the security guard.

There was a buzz and a click and the door swung open. Theo walked straight up to the security guard who sat behind the reception desk.

"I'm here to see..."

"Yes, that's right. Take the lift up to the third floor. You'll be met."

"Is this place open all the time?" Theo couldn't help asking.

"Yep! Seven days a week. Twenty-four hours a day," the guard replied.

Theo headed over to the lift. DemTech was nothing if not efficient! He pressed the button to go up to the third floor, speculating about what Bullet and his dad wanted to say to him. The lift doors slid open with a hiss.

"Hello. Theo, isn't it?" Jo Fleming stood right in front of the lift, a notepad in her hand.

"Hello, Miss Fleming," Theo said,

surprised. "I was meant to meet Bullet, I mean Toby, and his dad here."

"Oh, yes. Darius mentioned it. They've gone up to one of the labs on the seventh floor," said Jo. "I'll take you up."

Jo led the way to the lift and they headed up to the top floor in silence. Theo struggled to find something to say, but failed. He glanced at Jo, who had a preoccupied look on her face. Theo used the opportunity to scrutinize her. She was a dark horse and no mistake. Theo knew she'd been at DemTech for quite a few years now. He couldn't help wondering just what she really thought of her boss. Darius Marriott didn't seem like exactly the easiest man in the world to get along with. For a start, this woman always seemed to be working. It was Saturday and she was still in the office. Didn't she have a private life? Even when Theo was a great detective, he'd still make sure he had time for a personal life and to have some fun. Otherwise what was the point?

"Here we are," said Jo.

Theo stepped out into an eerie silence

which was a total contrast to the noise and organized chaos present when Darius Marriott had showed them around.

"Is it always this quiet on a Saturday?" Theo asked.

"No, not usually. Most of the quality assurance and testing staff work on Saturdays and some work on Sundays, too. It's just that most people are at the company knees-up tonight," Jo replied as they walked down the corridor. "I'm just on my way there now. Here we are. Bullet's in there."

Theo opened the door and walked in. "Hi, Bullet. What was so...?"

The door banged shut behind him. Theo spun around – but he was too late. With a resounding click, the door was locked.

19. No Way Out

"What on earth...? What's the matter?" Bullet asked urgently.

"Jo's locked the door," Theo replied. He started rattling the door handle. "Let us out! LET US OUT NOW!"

"Don't worry, Theo. We're going to deal with Toby – and then it's your turn," Jo called through the locked door.

"What d'you mean?" Theo's blood ran liquid nitrogen cold. "OPEN THIS DOOR."

"Sorry, Theo, but you've left us no choice. If what we've got lined up for Bullet doesn't work for you too, Ron's got a little something waiting for you on – or should I say off – the roof of this building."

"Jo, the joke's over. Let us out – *please*. Come on! You can't do this..." Theo pulled even harder on the door handle, but it was useless.

Beyond the door there was now nothing but an eerie silence. Theo shook the door handle, wondering if there was some way to force it open. Nothing doing! There was no way a big, heavy security door like that was going to give, no matter what Theo did to it.

"What's going on? What's she up to?" asked Bullet.

"I have a horrible feeling I know," Theo said through gritted teeth. "But I don't understand... Bullet, why did you want to see me?"

Bullet looked puzzled. "What're you talking about? You left a message with my mum saying that you wanted to see me at the DemTech building. You said it was a matter of life and death."

"But that's the message *I* got – that you wanted to see me," said Theo.

And all at once, it became very clear what was going on.

"Bullet," Theo fumed. "Ricky and I found out that Jo Fleming and Ron Westall are married. According to the old will, if anything should happen to your dad, combined they'd have enough shares to take over the company."

"But then Dad changed his will..." Bullet breathed. Realization like Antarctic water flowed over him.

"And they know that I've spent the day at the Family Records Centre finding out that the two of them are married. And d'you remember what else the DemTech stock contract said? If by any chance, any of the directors should even so much as live together, one of them would have to give up their shares, no arguments, no questions."

"But why lock us in here? They can't keep us here forever. We'll just shout until someone lets us out."

"Everyone's away at the summer party, so we won't be found until tomorrow. And I think Jo and Ron have got more than an overnight stay locked in this lab lined up for us."

"Oh, great! I am in BIG trouble. Mum's going to do her nut if I come home late again."

"Your mum! What about my mum and dad? Dad gave me strict instructions to be home early tonight. And Ricky's going to come round and I'm not going to be there."

Theo and Bullet looked around the empty lab. He looked up. Directly above them was the roof – but there was no way out to it from here. The vent high up on the wall was too high to reach and much too small to crawl through.

"What now?" Bullet asked.

"I guess we sit tight and wait for someone to let us out," Theo replied.

"But why on earth would she lock us in here in the first place?"

Theo walked around the lab looking for something, anything that would help him to prise open the door. Four computer terminals sat on the large table against the far wall and on the middle table were various electronic components, most of which Theo had never seen before and none of which could be used on the door.

"It's getting hot." Theo tugged at the neck of his sweatshirt. What had Jo done? Turned off the air conditioning? She must've done. The temperature in the room seemed to be leaping up. "Aren't you going to pull off your jumper?"

Bullet shook his head. "I'm cold."

"You're kidding! I'm sweltering."

"Yes, but... Oh-oh! I think the heat is the least of our problems. Look!" Bullet pointed up at the ventilation grille high above their heads. Theo looked up and saw a wasp crawl out of the grille and sit on it for a moment. Then out came another one. Then another. And another. Soon the grille was heaving with wasps, sitting on the grille, buzzing angrily. Theo turned to look at Bullet, who edged backwards away from the wasps until his back was against the wall and he had nowhere else to go. Theo started edging backwards, too. More and more wasps were coming out of the grille now, buzzing in shared fury.

Theo ran for the door. He rattled the handle frantically. "LET US OUT! SOMEONE, PLEASE! LET US OUT!"

"Theo, no. Don't shout or jump up and down," Bullet called out to him.

The wasps were on the move now. In twos and threes and fours they left the grille to begin flying around the room. Theo ran back to Bullet.

"Bullet, where's your hypo of adrenaline?"

"It's in my bag," Bullet said slowly.

"Where's your bag?" Theo desperately looked around the lab. "Bullet, where's your bag?" he repeated when Bullet didn't answer.

"It's under Jo's desk. She said I should leave it there for safe-keeping," Bullet whispered.

Theo stared at his friend, horror-stricken. "I never should've come up here with Jo. I knew it was her and Ron – so why did I do it? How could I have been so stupid?"

"You weren't to know," Bullet dismissed quickly.

"But I did know. Jo was the only one in the school hall with Darius when he visited our school. We knew that if the Lazarus suit malfunction was triggered by remote control using a computer, the computer would still have to be quite close. Jo Fleming is the only one who could've possibly done it. She must've had a laptop or one of those hand-held computers. Faith was too far away in a car outside the school grounds. I had all the pieces, I just didn't put them together."

"Never mind Jo. What about us?" Bullet, voice was stiff with fear.

More and more wasps emerged from the grille and took flight.

Theo pulled off his sweatshirt. "Quick! Wrap this around your head and stuff your hands in your pockets."

"No, Theo." Bullet shook his head. "If you get stung by this many wasps it could kill you, too."

"But just one sting could kill you. I'll take my chances."

"I can't let you do..."

"Bullet, we haven't got time for this," Theo protested impatiently. "Put this around your head. Come on."

Reluctantly, Bullet wrapped the sweatshirt around his head, leaving only a very little of his face exposed. Theo glanced down at his shirt and trousers. Suddenly they seemed as flimsy as tissue paper.

"I'll try and break one of the windows." Theo picked up a stool.

"But Dad said..."

"Any better ideas?"

Bullet shut up. Theo ran over to the window by the door and holding the stool with two hands, he heaved it at the glass. The stool bounced off the window, sending a shooting pain straight up Theo's arms. Ignoring the pain dancing around his shoulders, Theo tried again. And a third time. It was futile. The stool was coming off worse than the window. Theo dropped the stool in disgust.

"We'd both better get under that table," he announced.

"Wasps can fly under tables as well as over them, you know."

"It's better than nothing," Theo replied, pulling Bullet after him. "Come on. Hurry!" Theo was having to shout over the noise of the wasps in the lab now. And still they kept coming. Theo and Bullet knelt down under the computer table, both watching the grille. The wasps in the lab had to number at least one hundred and probably a lot more. Theo felt numb with fright. He'd never felt anything like it before, even when confronted with Angela's brother Tom and his so-called friends at the Irving Museum. Goodness knew he'd been scared enough then but this was much, much worse. Because Bullet was with him and Bullet was allergic to wasp stings and his adrenaline hypodermic syringe was outside the lab. It was only four floors below them but it might as well have been on the moon. Every time Theo had been in trouble before, it was down to him to find some way out. He could run or hide or call the police and although he'd been in some dangerous situations, there'd always been some way out. But not now. They were stuck in a lab full of wasps and the glass was toughened and the door was locked. There was no way out. What would happen if Bullet got stung? Theo knew the answer to that one and that was the trouble.

A wasp buzzed near his face. Theo swatted out with his hand to push it away.

"Don't do that. You'll just antagonize them more," Bullet whispered.

Theo dropped his hand at once. "Cover your face, Bullet. Quick, before – OW!" Theo snatched his hand off the floor and cradled it against his body. Already a lump was forming on his forearm around the wasp's sting.

Bullet pulled the sweatshirt off his face. "Theo, are you OK?"

"BULLET, SHUT UP AND COVER YOUR FACE," Theo yelled. "OWW! OUCH!"

The air was thick with wasps now. Theo couldn't see across the room and for all his big talk he wasn't sure how many more stings he could take.

"Theo, Jo's not going to open this door until I'm out of the way." Bullet pulled the sweatshirt off his face and spoke behind his hand. "With me out of the way, you stand a chance of escaping."

Bullet crawled out from under the table

and took Theo's sweatshirt off completely. Theo sprang after him.

"Bullet, are you out of your mind? Get back under..."

But Theo was too late. Wasps surrounded them like shrouds. Theo could feel stings like red hot pinches up and down his body. It was swelteringly hot in the room and getting hotter all the time and his skin felt like fires were breaking out all over it. But that wasn't the worst of it. Bullet was in trouble. He was surrounded by wasps.

"Can't ... breathe..." Bullet choked out, pulling at the neck of his jumper and the shirt underneath.

Theo rugby tackled Bullet to the floor and half pushed, half dragged him back under the table. He swatted out in every direction, trying to keep the wasps away from Bullet, oblivious to the stings they gave him in his desperation to help his friend.

"Bullet? Toby, speak to me. Are you all right?"

What a stupid question. Bullet's face and hands were puffed up like balloons and his lips and eyelids were horribly swollen. Theo grabbed hold of Bullet's wrist, searching for a pulse – and not finding one. His fingers darted back and forth over the inside of Bullet's wrist. Nothing. Theo felt for a pulse in Bullet's neck but he wasn't sure exactly where to press his fingers. He knocked the wasps off Bullet's jumper and put his ear down to Bullet's chest. Nothing. And that's when Theo knew. Bullet's heart had stopped beating.

Theo's whole body was on fire now. He was pain personified. And the buzzing... If only the buzzing would stop. Theo closed his eyes, his head still resting on Bullet's chest. He had to do something to escape from the intense, white-hot pain lancing up and down his body. He'd close his eyes. That's what he'd do. He'd close his eyes and allow himself to sleep, to move outside and beyond his body where the pain couldn't reach him.

A small part of Theo's mind told him not to sleep. To stay awake. To fight. But he couldn't. He was in agony and it was driving him crazy. If he didn't escape and soon, he wouldn't escape at all. Just to close his eyes, to allow his mind to drift away from his body... Theo did just that. And his last conscious thought was that Bullet was dead and he was dying.

20. Live Saver

It was the smell that hit Theo first. An antiseptic, disinfectant smell which instantly told Theo that he was in hospital. But he couldn't remember why. He struggled to open his eyes and the instant they were open he saw them. Hundreds and hundreds of them. Thousands and thousands of them. Wasps. Theo cried out. And they were instantly gone.

"Theo? It's all right, darling. Mum and Dad are here. You're OK now."

Theo looked over at the anguished faces of his parents. "I'm in hospital." It was a statement not a question.

"That's right." Theo's dad tried to smile, his eyes shimmering.

As Theo became more awake, he was aware of his head pounding like a woodpecker's beak. He tried to raise his hand to his head but, startled, he saw that it was swathed in bandages. Only then did he remember everything.

"Bullet. Where's Bullet? We have to help him. He..."

"Theo, calm down. Toby's fine. In fact he's in better shape than you are. He was only stung a couple of times on his hands and once on his face. The rest of his body was very well padded and protected."

"But he's allergic. One sting alone can kill him," Theo said, anguished.

"Yes, but he was well wrapped up to disguise the fact that he was wearing one of his dad's prototype Lazarus suits. He'd added his adrenaline syringe to the suit and it saved his life. Apparently he's been wearing it for the last couple of days – just in case."

"The Lazarus suit? Why didn't he say?"

"You'll have to take that up with him," Theo's mum said, an edge to her voice. "Ricky and Toby told me what's been happening from their point of view but now I want to hear it from you. I want to know exactly what you've been up to – from the beginning."

Theo kept his explanation as short as he could, but at the end of it he was still exhausted. But not too exhausted to catch the look exchanged between his parents.

"Theo, this must stop. If you get involved in something like this again, I want you to give me your word that you'll come to me or your mother and you'll tell us what's going on."

"But I was never in any real danger – not until we were locked in the lab with the wasps, at any rate," Theo argued.

"Yes, but look what happened then," said Theo's dad at once. "You were stung more than twenty times and if Mr Marriott's detective hadn't been on the spot, it might've been a lot, lot worse."

"Mr Marriott's what? His detective?" asked Theo.

"Apparently Mr Marriott appointed detectives to protect you, Ricky and Toby after Angela had her accident. He was worried that something else might happen."

Theo digested this piece of news. So he'd been right. There *had* been someone following him – but the man had been on his side.

"The man looking after you managed to drag you and Toby out of that lab just in time."

"What about the detective hired to look after Bullet? He should've been able to let us out of the lab almost immediately." Theo frowned. "Where was he?"

"He'd been knocked out by Ron and locked in the gents' toilets," said Dad.

"He was a fat lot of use then," Theo sighed, closing his eyes at the waves of fatigue washing over him. "So Toby's OK? You're sure?"

"Positive."

"What about Jo Fleming and Ron Westall?" Theo struggled not to succumb to his exhaustion. He wanted to know what had happened to the ones who'd done this to him.

"They've both been arrested and charged.

And it's only a matter of time before the police get the man they hired to get rid of Darius."

"So they didn't try to do that bit themselves?"

"No. Jo has confessed to everything. Apparently, they needed someone who could pretend to be a doctor and give Darius Marriott his fatal injection. Darius would've recognized both of them at once. Besides..."

Theo didn't hear any more. His eyes, already as heavy as lead weights, closed of their own accord and he was out of it.

"Hello. How're you feeling?"

Theo forced himself to focus on Ricky's voice. "I'm OK. How do I look?"

"D'you really want me to answer that?"

Theo sighed and sat up. "That bad, huh?"

"That bad and worse," Ricky stated. "Can I sit on your bed?"

"Yeah! No problem."

Ricky perched at the edge of the bed, pushing with his feet against the floor to steady himself.

"Where're my mum and dad?"

"They've gone to get something to eat. They've barely left your side in over twenty-four hours."

"Twenty-four hours?" Theo asked, aghast. "Have I really been out that long?"

Ricky nodded.

"So is it true? Have Jo Fleming and Ron Westall been arrested? Are they really the ones responsible for all this?"

"That's right. Of course I knew it was Jo when she said she'd been standing at the back of the assembly hall when Darius came to visit our school. She was the only one close enough to set off the Lazarus suit by remote control."

"Yeah, I figured that out as well – but almost too late." Theo wondered what had happened to his brain over the last couple of days. He should've been able to work that out a lot sooner. It was obvious. "What made you suspect that Jo wasn't working alone, though?"

"You didn't see her face when she introduced us to Ron at the DemTech offices. She was looking at him the way your mum and dad look at each other and he was looking back in exactly the same way. And then she started rubbing the ring finger of her left hand – even though she didn't have on a wedding ring."

"You're joking!"

"No, I'm not. She wasn't aware that she was doing it, but I noticed. And it made me wonder. And once I knew they were married then we had a motive right there. Their combined shares would give them control of the company once Darius was out of the way," said Ricky. "And Bullet told me that Ron had been dead set against Darius's Lazarus suit idea from the beginning. Ron thought it was a waste of money."

"It saved Bullet's life," Theo pointed out.

"Yes, it did," Ricky said thoughtfully. "He snaffled one from an empty lab that day he left his duffle bag behind."

"So he left his bag behind on purpose," Theo realized.

Ricky nodded.

"Where's Bullet now?"

"In the ward across the corridor. He's going to visit you a little later."

Theo raised his eyebrows. "Is he up and about already?"

"Yep! The doctors reckon he can go home tomorrow at the latest."

Theo leaned back against the pillows. He felt strangely ... flat. The whole world had moved off and up and on without him. Jo and Ron had been arrested and he hadn't seen it. Bullet was going to be all right and he hadn't witnessed it. He was out of things. It wasn't a very comforting feeling.

"At least you're doing well, Ricky. You're the only one of our group who isn't in hospital," Theo laughed.

Ricky didn't join in.

"What's the matter?" Theo asked, his smile fading.

"I should've been there," Ricky exploded. "I knew what might happen. I should've been there. That's why I told you not to leave the house without me, but you went anyway. You ... you could've been killed."

Theo stared at Ricky, who was more

distraught than Theo had ever seen him. "Ricky, look at me. I'm OK. I could've been killed but I wasn't."

"Yes, but you..."

"Ricky, I'm fine. I promise," Theo insisted. Ricky's mouth snapped shut. He didn't look very happy, nor particularly convinced but he stopped arguing. "So what will happen to Ron and Jo now?"

Ricky shrugged. "Bullet told me that his dad wanted the police to drop the charges but nothing doing."

"Drop the charges?" Theo stared at Ricky. "Has Mr Marriott lost his mind?"

"No. Mr Marriott has lost something a great deal more precious to him," said Ricky.

"What d'you mean?"

"I think Mr Marriott has been dipping into his company's reserves to finance his Lazarus suit. I think DemTech isn't worth as much as everyone thinks it is."

"What makes you think that? And since when were you interested in financial goings-on?"

"Since we became involved in this whole

business," Ricky replied. "D'you remember when Mr Marriott told us that the Lazarus suit cost over twenty million in development last year alone?"

"Yes. So?"

"Last year DemTech reported profits of just over twelve million. That's what I went to the library to check," said Ricky.

"And if he hadn't spent the twenty million on the suit it would've been thirty-two million instead." Theo frowned. "What's your point?"

"In the official accounts and the shareholders reports, DemTech is down as having spent only seven million on R&D throughout the whole company in the last year," said Ricky. "I think Mr Marriott accidentally let slip to us what the real cost was."

"Well, he can afford it." Theo still didn't see what the problem was.

"But can he?" Ricky said. "I think that in their own twisted way, Ron and Jo were right. I think that Darius has been dipping into his own company's funds in order to finance the

R&D on his Lazarus suit. I reckon that's why he wanted to drop the charges against Ron and Jo, because otherwise there might be external auditors and all sorts going through the company's books to see just what's been going on."

"But as company treasurer, wouldn't Ron have known all about it?"

"Not necessarily. I think he more than suspected," said Ricky. "That's probably why he wanted to stop Darius – before Darius bankrupted the entire company."

"But what proof do you have of all this?" Theo asked.

"Yes, I'd be very interested to hear that, too."

Theo's and Ricky's heads snapped around. Darius Marriott was standing right behind them. Theo looked around him but luckily Darius was alone.

"Go on, Ricky. I'd like to hear how you intend to prove what you've just said," said Darius.

Ricky didn't answer. Both he and Theo sat perfectly still, watching Darius Marriott with unblinking eyes. Darius looked around the ward before turning back to the two boys.

"Because I'll tell you now," said Darius. "It's all perfectly true. I've been borrowing money from the DemTech pension fund and from my company's staff saving scheme to invest in my new invention. But if you go to the police now, DemTech will go down the drain and Toby's future will go right along with it. In a few months' time, once my Lazarus suit is on the market, I'll be able to replace every penny I've taken and no one will be any the wiser. So I'll ask you again, what d'you intend to do about it?"

"You deliberately changed your will knowing that the person or people after you would go after Bullet instead," Ricky said quietly. "You put your own son in the firing line, whilst you hid behind him."

Darius's lips tightened. "I hired private detectives to protect him – to protect all of you."

"But you wouldn't have had to do any of that if you hadn't changed your will in the first place," Ricky pointed out. "From the moment I heard you'd done that, I knew what kind of father you were. I knew what kind of man you were. I knew you had to be mixed up in something shady because you're incapable of doing anything else. You don't care about Toby any more than you care about the stranger in the next bed. Toby was just a convenient decoy. Someone you could use to get the people who'd tried to kill you out into the open."

Theo sat frozen to the bed. He couldn't believe what he was hearing and yet every word Ricky uttered clicked into place and made perfect sense.

"Spare me the lecture please. I'll ask you again. What d'you intend to do about it?" Darius repeated icily.

Ricky looked at Theo, then back at Darius Marriott. "Nothing," he said, softly. "I'm not going to be the one to tell Toby what his dad really is. I'm not going to be the one to tell him that his dad doesn't care a kidney bean about him."

A slow smile spread across Darius's face, as if he'd expected no other answer. Theo longed to yell at him, shout out to the whole ward and the whole world just what Darius Marriott had done. But he knew he wouldn't.

"Hello, Dad. Hi, Ricky, Theo," Bullet called out from a few beds away as he strode up the middle of the ward.

"Hi, son." Darius gave Ricky and Theo a look of pure triumph before he turned to Bullet. "How're you feeling?"

"I'm fine. I'm more worried about Theo. He covered my body with his to stop me being stung. He saved my life."

"I think my Lazarus suit did that, Toby," Darius laughed.

"That as well!" Bullet agreed. "I owe my life to Angela, Theo and your Lazarus suit respectively! So Theo, are you OK?"

"I'm fine." Was that really his voice? So distant?

"You don't sound it!" Bullet said, concerned.

Theo forced himself to smile, and forced the smile into his voice. "Toby, I'm fine."

"Now I know you're not. You've never called me Toby in your life!" said Bullet.

Ricky and Theo looked at each other and grinned.

"I'll never be able to thank you for what you did for me," Bullet added, looking embarrassed. "You're a good friend. Both of you, and Angela – and I won't forget it."

"Bullet, if you're going to get all mushy, I'll turn my head, shall I?" asked Ricky. "Then you can give Theo a kiss without my seeing it."

"Ricky, why don't you...?"

"Toby!" Darius admonished.

"...Go and play in the traffic!" Bullet finished.

"Bullet, just remember Ricky, Angela and I will always be your friends – OK?" Theo couldn't help saying.

"OK." Bullet grinned happily.

Theo looked up at Darius. Something told him that with a father like Darius Marriott, Bullet was going to need all the friends he could get. But for now, it was over and Bullet was safe. And at that moment, that was all that mattered.